Penitent's Gold

Terrace V

Penitent's Gold

Purgatorio Towers #5

Curated by

Sarah L. Pratt & Robert Bose

Illustrated by

Aaron Bilawchuck

THE SEVENTH TERRACE

TERRACE V: PENITENT'S GOLD
ISBN 13: 978-1-990082-20-7
The Seventh Terrace First Trade Paperback Edition - 2022

The Seventh Terrace
www.the-seventh-terrace.com

For the poets.

DREAMS OF AVARICE

WELCOME

GARY

Dear newly arrived Penitents—greetings and welcome!

By now you've begun to admire your opulent rooms and suites, newly renovated with Purgatorial quartz countertops and luxury vinyl plank flooring. Each exquisite, each unique, and while you rage in greedy desire to fill it with all manner of lavish accoutrements, understand that you must book the elevator for all deliveries and that failing to do so inevitably brings the wrath of the hagfish slumbering in the conduits.

In lighter news, the tenacious malignancy infesting our wretched backwater of a celestial halfway house has settled into an endemic coexistence with the many curses and maladies already in residence. With this now behind us, I'm pleased to announce all mandates and restrictions have been lifted, even the ones you have come to rely on for your daily amusement. And yes, dine-in is once again available at Nihilist Arby's—at the risk of your immortal souls and stomach membranes (for those with traditional stomachs).

And before I forget, because frankly I couldn't give a flying fuck, I have been requested by Jan, your Terrace V floor representative and spoken word berserker, to remind you all that the Winter Solstice Poetry Slam will be held this coming Wednesday evening at the morning lava ponds and that participation by all floor reps is mandatory.

(There Jan, I made your announcement, now get off my neck.)

Gary

President
Purgatory Towers Tenant's Association

WINTER SOLSTICE POETRY SLAM

TENANT ASSOCIATION

So, yeah, it's the Third Wednesday of the Twelfth Month of the Year of the Seeping Centipede, of the Century of the Diseased Fruit Bat, of the Millennium of the Factory Supersale, and you know what that means? If you said Winter Solstice Poetry Slam you win only my contempt, but you'd be correct!

All floor reps are required to go head-to-head, poetically (most forms recognized, some more recognized than others), in a spoken word throwdown for Factory gift certificates (first prize) and bragging rights (honorable mention), between which a duly appointed scribe from the hallowed halls of Terrace V will regale us with a tale of avarice as a palate cleanser. Losers are given the choice between having their talentless hides singed off in the morning lava ponds or spending a night in the cruel malodorous embrace of our fearless President, may he live forever and ever and ever. Blah, blah, blah.

Jesus, are we really doing this? Yeah…so, it's not a joke…fine…I said *fine*. Gods…I swear the second I pay off my student loans…

Now on with the show!!

\- Arya Hermione Everdeen
Master of Ceremonies
Gen Z Chickadee
Unpaid Intern to Jan

GOLD DIGGER

TAIJA MORGAN

By the time the funeral is in progress, Jennifer is composed and plans to stay that way. Caleb drops her off curbside, doesn't join her. Part of her wishes he would have, just to see their faces. From the funeral home's office, she listens to voices echoing off the pristine marble floor in the lobby. They close in — sharper, louder, the click of high heels reverberating. Jennifer takes a deep breath, holds it, schools her face. The mahogany door opens.

"You've got to be kidding me. His whore? The nerve."

Jennifer doesn't turn her head as Barbara stalks into the room. She recognizes the woman's voice from about a million overheard voicemail messages. *I know you're out with her, Max. You think I don't know what you're doing?*

The spitting vitriol is no different in person. And frankly, Jennifer craves it the way she craves a cigarette between her lips right now. The low tremble of unbridled *hurt* in the woman's voice makes her seem out of control, weak. She bares her pain for everyone to see like an injured deer, limping through a field with an arrow in its back. Jennifer always did like the part where Bambi's mom died the best. Even better, the woman doesn't seem to know Max has changed his will—and cut Barbara out of it.

Jennifer sits up straighter in the wingback chair, smooths out her black Valentino dress—which, by the way, was featured in Cosmo's article *How Not to Look Like a Slut at a Funeral,* so she's feeling pretty confident in her choice. Retail: $7000. A modest cut, high neck, low leg, because ultimately this is a business meeting. The dress had been a gift from Max, along with the Louboutin heels and a tasteful Gucci Dionysus bag with Swarovski crystal accents. Little did either of them know at the time that she'd be wearing the ensemble to his funeral.

Barbara takes a seat to Jennifer's left, shoots a side-eyed glare over her shoulder, but if looks could kill Barb's husband would have croaked decades ago. The grieving widow's uniform: faux veil, Yves Saint Laurent Opyum slingback pumps, a severe silk Chanel dress, all black. Plunging V-neck, though, because those suckers cost ten times what Jennifer paid for her first car and no one puts Baby in a corner.

Behind her, Max's two grown kids trail in. Sterling and Celina. The latter clutching a white lambskin heart-shaped Chanel bag, gold chain strap. Retail: $6,500. Matching sandals. A satin and tulle Simone Rocha dress, very much this season. All white — almost bridal. An odd choice for the day of a funeral, but it still provokes a flicker of indignation in Jennifer at not having thought of this particular power move herself. Genius.

Celina was the least favoured of Maximillian's two brats. The way she slams that Chanel bag on the desk before sitting says it all and more. A scowl puckers her lips. Sterling is wearing an Armani suit, simple lines, a casual "sure, I'm grieving, but I have to catch the next flight to Ibiza with the boys" vibe that Jennifer doesn't hate. Handsome, like his father.

The lawyer strides in next. Grey hair pulled back in a low bun. Vapid and unmemorable. Max had specifically requested the reading of the will to occur right before the wake — a sure-fire way to spark an explosion of drama. Intentional, no doubt. He'd have loved this. The thought leaves her oddly empty, but she shakes it off.

Jennifer's ready to look surprised at the announcement, planning an open-mouthed O shaping her coral lips, paired with raised, perfectly arched brows, a quivering hand to her chest to really sell it. *What, it's all for me? Oh my, I had no idea, I'm so overwhelmed...*

The lawyer adjusts her glasses and time stretches languidly in the air between them. A tense silence grips the space as the lawyer clears her throat and begins the reading of Max's will.

Celina is the first to snap. "What the hell am I supposed to do with a house in Malibu? I told him I wanted the villa in Italy! Doesn't anyone care what *I* want?"

The twenty-five-year-old's shrill voice leaves the room's stained-glass windows vibrating. Technically, Celina has a year on Jennifer—a point of irritation on the girl's part—but she has nothing in actual life experience, looks like a toddler playing dress-up in Mommy's closet.

"Celina, please," the lawyer intones. To the young man next to Celina, she says, "Sterling, your father left you his prized car collection."

"Oh great," the boy mumbles, thumbing his iPhone screen, "the upkeep on that alone will bankrupt me. Typical."

The lawyer's French-tipped nail runs down the paper. "And the rest of Max's estate goes to…"

Jennifer's breath catches as a future laden with yachts and summer houses sprawls out before her.

"…his spouse, Barbara."

The declaration hits Jennifer like a bucket of cold water over her head. She doesn't have to orchestrate the dropped jaw or the raised brows. "W-what?" She's on her feet in an instant, composure abandoned as her heart trips into a gallop.

"Did you expect something else?" Barbara asks. A slow grin crawls across the woman's wrinkled lips.

Jennifer's hands clench at her sides. "Th-that's wrong, i-it's supposed to be … he —"

Barbara flutters a silk handkerchief in front of her face, throws her head back like she's in a period drama. "Will someone remove her, please? Honestly, no one has any consideration for my poor nerves!"

All eyes turn to Sterling. He glances up from his phone, shrugs, and stands, reaching for Jennifer's bicep.

She jerks away. "You can't do this!" Her voice is too high now, the slap of the news still resounding. "Max and I … we were in love."

"You need to leave," the lawyer says.

But she *can't*. "I-I have a right to say goodbye to him, as much as anyone."

Sterling's loose hand falls away. He looks to his mother, his sister, the lawyer.

The lawyer stands. "The body is in the viewing room. You have five minutes."

Okay, *love* may have been an overstatement. What Jennifer and Max shared was an investment, and really, what was love if not an investment? She'd done her part. And in the end, the fucker screwed her over. The house, the bank accounts, the investment properties, the 401k, they should all be hers. Fair compensation for her *considerable* labour.

In the viewing room, a handful of mourners are gathered to say their goodbyes, mostly standard-fair old white guys with the occasional Stepford wife. The undulating wave of black dresses and suits parts around Jennifer as she enters. The room smells sweet, a potent mixture of flowers, cologne, and a few swirling tumblers of bourbon in the mourners' hands. Lilies and roses are stacked high near the platform where Max's coffin rests, and are those—? They are. Carnation wreathes. How unexpectedly pedestrian. The florist must have made a mistake, or perhaps the funeral director allowed some of the common rabble to send their condolences. He was a popular man, after all—respected and feared, if not loved. But he'd have hated those carnations, and so she hates them for him.

Jennifer shoves past the other mourners and strides up to the coffin. Hot tears burn her eyes when she sees him.

You bastard. You goddamned bastard.

It isn't fair. Blinking hard, she glances around. Eyes flicker her way, pretending they aren't watching. A shed tear would sell this well, but she can't do it—didn't wear the waterproof mascara today, a massive oversight.

She turns her gaze back to Max. He looks more alive than the last time she'd been with him, a red dye mixed with the embalming fluid replicating the effect of blood flowing through his veins. So realistic, she could reach out and touch his cheek, expecting it to still be warm. But he's so still, so impossibly still, that something in her guts revolts at the thought.

He lounges in a handcrafted, solid bronze coffin with velvet interior and gold-plated detailing. The Cadillac of burial options. Thirty thousand dollars they were shoving in the ground right there. And for what? A pretty box for Max to rot in. Her stomach is a sunken pit as she takes him in.

It's an uncommon choice, the six-sided coffin over a standard rectangular casket—no doubt custom-made—but the tapered shape makes his shoulders seem broader, a touch statelier, and Jennifer wonders if he could have planned that somehow. If he has planned every tiny detail of this day to play out exactly the way he wants, even if he's not around to see it.

He's wearing a single-breasted wool and mohair Prada suit. Another $4,600. Salvatore Ferragamo plain-toe oxfords in polished calfskin leather, clocking in at a mere $1,900. And was that—? Yes, eighteen karat gold Dolce & Gabbana cufflinks with inlaid rubies and a matching tie bar. An easy six grand.

Jennifer's breath catches. They couldn't possibly be burying him in the cufflinks. His wedding ring is there, too. And on his left wrist, just the flash of something gold under his cuff.

With a quick glance side to side, she snakes her hand into the casket, tugs at his sleeve. His favourite gold Rolex. Retail: $130,000. The room spins.

Behind her, Barbara's venomous voice says, "Time's up, you gold-digging whore."

A set of strong arms drag her away from Max's body.

Jennifer packs bolt cutters, but they don't end up needing them. Larry, the security guy, is an easy bribe. Jennifer's flashlight illuminates the rich green sod overlaying Max's fresh grave. Caleb carries the shovel and a backpack.

"This is it." Jennifer stamps out a cigarette as she stares up at the tall granite pillar marking Max's final resting place. The rose-hued stone sparkles with dew. She pulls her leather jacket tighter.

"A watch can't truly be worth this—this … violation, *amore*." Caleb scratches at the stubble along his sharp jaw, his brown eyes serious.

She huffs in his direction. "Trust me, it is."

"How much are we talking about, then?"

Jennifer hesitates. She's not sure why. But they're in this together, so he might as well know. "One hundred and thirty."

"Dollars?"

"*Thousand* dollars."

Caleb stumbles backward a step. "You really think they buried him with it? Surely they'd have removed it after the viewing."

Jennifer doesn't know for certain, but something burns in her chest and maybe it's hatred or rage or nerves, but whatever it is, she needs to exorcise it and can't stop until she does.

"Only one way to find out. Help me roll the sod back."

Caleb drops the backpack and the shovel next to the granite pillar. Together they pull at the grass seam, rolling the unrooted earth back like a heavy blanket. The surrounding grass is still trampled from the crowd this afternoon, a soiled tissue crushed into the ground near the pillar.

"You sure about this, amore?" Caleb wipes at his forehead, though the air is chilled. "Seems a bit … morbid, no?"

"He owes it to me."

"What if the body is all, you know, rotting and stinking?"

"It won't be. He was just embalmed."

"I just mean, does it have to be today? Couldn't we think on it a little while? If the watch isn't even there…"

Jennifer doesn't answer him. This is the best shot they've got, the loosest the dirt will ever be, the best Max will ever smell. Jennifer grabs the shovel and holds it out to Caleb.

Caleb raises his hands, shaking his head. "Oh, no, no. I cannot. My carpel tunnel."

Jennifer frowns.

Caleb steps forward, placing his hands on either side of her face and leaning in to kiss her forehead. "Don't be mad? I'll keep you company.

Serenade you with the poetry I've been working on."

Jennifer sighs. She sinks the shovel into the still soft earth and begins the slow, painstaking process of digging down to Max's dirt-clogged coffin.

Hours later, Caleb's voice is hoarse with his recitations and Jennifer is physically exhausted. The squelch of mud sucking at the shovel has worn her down. Dirt cakes beneath her broken nails, manicure ruined beyond repair. Her discarded jacket lay at the rim of the freshly dug grave high above her head, and severed worms litter the earthen walls of the hole, still wriggling.

Above her on the other side, a mountain of displaced earth threatens to spill back into the hole, a landslide waiting to happen that leaves her knees quaking with the risk. She flicks an ant off her arm, slaps another when its mandibles nip at her flesh, then hands the shovel back up to Caleb.

She fiddles with the locking mechanism at the base of the coffin until she hears it release, but the solid bronze lid is so heavy, her arms so rubbery, she'll need extra leverage. Standing astride the lid of Max's coffin, Jennifer calls up to Caleb, "I need the pry bar."

"*Sì.*"

Jennifer jumps as it lands with a clang against the metal lid beneath her. Lifting her filthy hand to her eyes, she can barely make out Caleb's shadowed form above her in the darkness, looming against the moon's dull light behind him. She shakes the stringy hair out of her face and grabs the bar, positioning it into the seam of the coffin lid and leaning all her weight into the awkward angle. There's an audible *pop* as the rubber gasket sealing the coffin releases.

With a loud groan, the coffin opens. Jennifer is breathing hard, panting both from the workout and from anticipation. She lifts the heavy lid, stepping over it in the too-tight space and registering just how deep she is, how dark this pit is, how close the walls are on either side of her and can she breathe—why can't she breathe? *Don't panic.*

Flicking on her flashlight, she directs the beam onto Max's dead face. He looks like he's sleeping, except there's no drool at the corner of his mouth and his chest doesn't rise or fall. For a moment, though, she thinks she sees it—a breath pushing up his ribcage.

Don't be stupid, she tells herself. It's only gases. His body is slowly eating itself, microbes and gut flora waging their last doomed battle, impeded by the embalming fluids but not halted completely. She'd interned with a mortician for a few years— she knew what to expect. That's how she knew Larry would let *anyone* do *anything* to a corpse for a bottle of whisky and a Cuban cigar. But still, she finds herself reaching down, fingers hovering a breath away from his cheek. Her own chest constricts as her fingertips glance over his skin, smearing the makeup there with grave dirt.

She jerks away and her stomach clenches.

Cold to the touch. But he'd never been a warm person.

"What do you see?" Caleb calls from a world away.

Jennifer blinks. Shakes her head. Swallows. "A dead man. Hand me the bag."

The backpack lands squarely on Max's face. Jennifer cringes but leaves it there. It isn't that she feels bad. But part of her wonders if he might open his eyes—can't bear to consider how the cloudy blue orbs would look in death, dull and flat, void of his vibrance, his mischievous spark. Just the thought leaves her throat tight.

She reaches first for Max's wrists, gratified beyond measure to see the glint of the gold cufflinks and, yes, there it is—the watch, still in place. All of this is suddenly worth it. Worth everything.

Her grin lifts her voice as she tells Caleb, "It's here! It's still here!" like she can't quite believe it herself. Caleb whoops above her, reinvigorated.

She slips the antiquated coin cufflinks free and palms them, leaving dirt on the pristine white fabric of his dress shirt. He'd have hated that. The skin beneath his cuffs is a sickly marbled hue, no makeup there to cover up what death really looks like.

Jennifer unzips a pocket of the bag and slides the cufflinks in. Easy. The matching tie bar goes next. This close to him, she can smell the metallic tang of the bronze coffin, the wet earth of the grave, and beneath, just a phantom edge of rot. It's her imagination, filling in the scent of rot where she subconsciously expects to find it, even though he's still freshly embalmed. Even imagined, she can't stop smelling it.

She catches a glimpse of something white and squirming in Max's exposed ear and she startles back with a gasp. But the flashlight reveals nothing. A trick of the light, or lack of it. She swallows down the bile at the back of her throat, trying not to think about maggots in Max's orifices, or the sensation of maggots wriggling under her own skin.

Inhaling deeply, she rolls up the cuff on Max's left wrist. Jennifer's fingertips dance across the icy-cold metal of the Rolex.

A chill flickers up her spine. $130,000. Tossed away in a grave like it was nothing. As if the dead had any use for it. It was Max's favourite, but it wasn't his most expensive watch—he had a few in the half-a-million range. But this one, he'd won it, cheating at a poker game. Gave him a certain extra thrill to wear, since he took it away from someone else. This was his walking-around watch. Something his family, clearly, wouldn't miss any more than they missed him.

She slides it off and adds it to the bag. It feels anticlimactic, despite the exhilaration sweeping through her veins now. The thrill isn't enough. No, she's not finished here. Not yet.

The flashlight glints off Max's wedding ring. Why they'd bury him with this, too, she can't fathom. It's like they don't want any part of him now. Not the way she does. His family had never really known him, only a curated version of him, a version crafted to perform for elaborate dinner parties and packed boardrooms. She wonders if she really knew him either, but then thinks, *Yes, I knew you. I did.* There were quiet moments between them that were too intimate to be faked, where even she was real and the masks were down. And that had been genuine, that intimacy. Only, maybe it was just real for her. After all, he'd manage to fuck her one last time with the will.

Jennifer runs her finger over the ring, unsure of its value. Solid gold, to be sure. Inlaid with diamonds. She tugs on the ring, but it doesn't budge.

He had never taken it off, not even during all the times he'd slid that finger inside her right up to the knuckle. She'd figured it was a subtle fuck-you to his wife, burying that warm metal in a hot twenty-four-year-old. Tugging on his finger now, she realizes the damn thing is just fused in place after so many years with the raging bitch.

Jennifer pulls as hard as she can. A popping sound makes her stomach churn, but she still can't free it.

She sits back on her haunches, crouched over his lower body like she had been so many times before. The last time she'd been this close to him, his heart had given out.

A thought struck her.

"Caleb, we packed those bolt cutters, right?"

"Amore?"

She pulls the bag toward her and rummages through it, not looking at Max's revealed face. "Never mind." Pulling the item out, Jennifer exhales. The humiliation from earlier in the day still stings, vivid and hot. She turns the bolt cutters over in her hand. *You bastard. You did this to yourself.*

Caleb's head peeks over the edge and the beam of his flashlight hits her, startlingly bright. She flinches, suddenly seeing herself being seen like this, hunched over the dead body of her lover, smeared in graveyard dirt. She squints against the glare, covering her eyes, shielding her gaze from meeting his.

When he lowers the beam, she sees his frown. "Bolt cutters?"

She lifts Max's heavy hand from where it rests over his chest, positions it. "The ring. It's stuck."

His eyes widen. "Just leave it," Caleb pleads, sounding distressed, as if her plan wasn't what was going to get them *both* set up with a new life in the city, help him get his poetry published.

"What?" She scowls. "Don't be ridiculous."

"We have what we came for."

Jennifer shakes her head, dirt-laden hair slapping her cheeks. His family didn't even want this ring. Buried it. As if they could throw it away. Throw him away. This ring should have been hers.

Her eyes fall on Max's now uncovered face. "No. It's mine." *He's mine.* She touches something inside herself then, a well of grief she hadn't expected beneath the indignant rage; fingers skimming the surface of that water, so cold, so deep. Her throat tightens and it's as if she feels his hand on her skin, brushing her neck, squeezing. *"I'm yours,"* she'd told him once in a whisper.

She swallows hard. Wills it away. It's not as if she loved him for real. This was just business. She shifts her center of gravity for the leverage, digging into the velvet cushioning on either side of him with her knees, bruises still aching there from the last time she'd knelt in front of him.

Holding tightly to Max's cold, stiff finger, Jennifer sinks the bolt cutters down. She doesn't look away from his face in case — god help her — he winces. But he doesn't.

The bone crunches. The finger comes partially away but not entirely. After all that digging, her grip is weak. She's forced to saw at it with the bolt cutters, pulling at the dangling flesh and muscle until the finger is finally free and his hand flops to his side. Bile burns the back of her throat again, and when she stops, she's shaking.

With trembling hands, she slips the ring off the dismembered finger and drops it into her palm.

It's beautiful, she realizes. She's never noticed that before. Not a designer brand she recognizes, but still … beautiful.

Settling the finger onto the velvet next to his head, she scoops up her flashlight and examines the gold band. Inscribed on the inside are the words *Amor Aeternus* — eternal love. Barbara must have chosen it, knowing Max's fondness for Latin. The thought sours Jennifer. Had it been Max's choice, Jennifer is sure he'd have used his favourite phrase, *amore et melle et felle es fecundissimus,* which he'd always wryly translated as *love is rich with honey and venom.* Far more fitting for their marriage.

Jennifer balances herself with one hand on his broad chest, wonders briefly about the trocar incision that would be hidden beneath his shirt just inches below her hand, where the mortician suctioned fluid out of his organs during the embalming process the way plastic surgeons liposuction fat.

Her lips are tingling, numb, as she calls up to Caleb, "I got it."

Caleb groans. "I can't do this any longer, amore. I'm done."

But she can't leave. It's not enough. "I think we could take the suit, too. The tie. The shoes. We should take it all."

"Jennifer," he says. "Don't you hear yourself?"

She tugs at Max's red Tom Ford tie, remembering the smooth silk beneath the pads of her thumbs the last time she'd tied it for him, the way he'd smirked at her as she straightened it. His stiff head lolls slightly to the side as the tie slips free. The smell of rot wafts up again.

Beneath the collar of his dress shirt, she can see the crude, thick stitches at his carotid where the embalming fluid was pumped into him. She'd seen it a thousand times, the process. But all she can think now is how Max had that extreme phobia of needles, how he even had to look away when she got a flu shot and nearly vomited in the parking lot after, and didn't anyone care about that? It's not as though he felt it. He was dead. He didn't feel anything. He couldn't have been *scared*.

Jennifer shakes her head, shoves the tie and the ring into the backpack and throws it up to Caleb. She hears him catch it, the sigh of relief that follows like a little kid stuck in a waiting room, finally able to leave. And they should. Leave, that is. She should leave.

Jennifer can't stop looking at the body though.

Distantly, she thinks about the coffin itself—solid bronze, and surely they could make some money off that—but no, it's far too heavy, a logistical nightmare. Max's titanium hip—could she get anything for that? No, those had serial numbers. Too hard to fence. If only she hadn't called the police when he'd croaked beneath her—surely some of those organs could have had value left in them. Stupid. Stupid to have trusted him, taken him at his word. What kind of idiot believes a mark when they tell you they've left you everything in their will? She knew better. Well, now she'd never make that mistake again. *Get paid upfront, sweetheart.* Max's boyish grin flashes through her mind, the glint of his gold tooth.

Gold tooth. Jennifer stills.

She squats again, reaches, thumb outlining the shape of Max's lips, pulling them back into a snarl. There it is. A gold canine. She thinks of his teeth sinking into the flesh of her shoulder, just enough to hurt, to mark, to push her over the edge. She bites her lip. How much would that tooth actually be worth? Compared to the watch, nothing. A pittance. But all of that, she'd sell, pawn, fence, whatever she could manage. Then what is she *left* with? She needs more. She needs *everything*.

Caleb's voice carries down again, but she can't make out his words through the blood rushing in her head. He sounds angry. She thinks he's saying something about the watch and a plane ticket and forgiveness.

She clears her throat. "I'm almost done."

Above her, grass rustles. Maybe he's leaving. But she can't leave. She won't. All she wants is a part of him. To keep. To hang on to. Something that was just his, no ties to his family, his wife, his business. Something that can be *hers*.

Her fingertips brush over his lips. Jaw in her hands, she tries to open his mouth but can't. Wired closed, for the wake.

She tugs his bottom lip down and sees it now, two wires anchored into his dry gums, top and bottom, like the bars of a cage. She knows what it feels like, to be caged. The hole around her seems small and tight as she thinks about it.

All she can smell is the heavy, musty scent of raw earth and that hint of rot, so overpowering she feels sick with it. She pulls her hand back but leans her head closer to Max's. Red ants march across the velvet near her mouth, mandibles snapping.

"I hate you," she tells him. Whispers it against his ear. Wonders if he'll hear her somehow and know she's lying. They'd always lied to each other.

The bolt cutters are bulky and too big, scraping against the enamel of his white teeth as she clips the two wires. Max's jaw falls open.

She tries to get the tooth now, snapping and pulling, but she can't get a grip on it with bolt cutters. She flips them upside down in her hand and smashes the butt of the tool into his teeth.

"I hate you," she spits, over and over, her chest as tight as the hole around her, slamming the bolt cutters into his mouth again and again, barely noticing the tears and sweat dripping onto his expensive suit. "I *hate* you."

A crack, and there it is. A gap in his crooked smile where more than one tooth is missing now and part of his upper jaw is caved in.

With a shuddering breath, her fingers dig around in his spongy mouth, desperately trying to capture the gold tooth at the back of his throat before it slips into his gullet.

She pinches the tooth between her fingers and pulls it out, wiping at her eyes with the back of her hand, sniffling.

"I got it!" She laughs then, and it bubbles up in her throat as she stands, holding the gold tooth up to her eyes. It gleams in the soft moonlight. It feels like deliverance. "I got it, Caleb! It's mine! It's … it's *mine*."

The crack of the shovel against her skull snaps her head back so hard that she hears a crunch, feels it like fire whipping through her whole body along the cable of her spine. She's lying on top of Max, staring up at the night sky, before she even notices Caleb standing high above her, shovel in his hands. Carpal tunnel? Not with that swing.

She tries to move, can't. That's when the fear hits. Sudden, like a dam breaking. She can't *move*.

"I'm sorry, amore," he's saying, a distant noise in her ringing ears. "I don't have a choice, can't you see? The money — it won't last split two ways. I need this. You see that I need this more, don't you? I just … I didn't want it to be this way, but how can I trust you…"

His words churn in her mind, crashing waves that break up into nothing. Beneath the swell of noise, she hears something else. A whisper near her ear, a cold breath that chills her, scalp to toes. Max's voice.

"Mine."

She tries to scream but she *can't move*. Short gasps rack her chest and tears leak out the corners of her eyes, dripping into her hair and onto Max beneath her. The gold tooth is cupped in her open palm. The first shovelful of dirt lands on her from above as the scent of rot rises once more and a cold hand with one missing finger tightens around her wrist.

PRIDE

Welcome to the SLAM! We're barely holding this rabid crowd back and the weather is perfectly wet and red, so let's get started. First up, we are "proud" to present our contestant from the ground level, a feline with a truly towering ego, oily hide, and a predator's instinct for rhyme and meter.

In the First Person
Performed by Cleo the Sphinx

I'm an artisan from an olden Pride
Where two large and legless Felines of stone
Lay in the desert… tails curled at their side
Half sunken their tattered whiskers outgrown

And their razored teeth, grinning cold and snide
Show I, their sculptor, knew their killer's souls
Which yet survive, trapped in these hardened sands
In still paws that toyed before lethal blows

And on their collars, engraving still clear
Cats rule and dogs drool, in all of your lands
Look on our works ye mighty and despair!
All that is left are the matted remains
A desiccated, disgorged ball of hair
Tumbling across the sands' lone level grains

Judges' Notes

- We kneel before our feline overlords!
- Such faithful adherence to the Petrachan/Shakespearean sonnet blend, which must have been a peculiar pain in the ass.
- Um, Percy Shelley here, Terrace II—
- Your objections are noted, Shelley.

Score: 9/10 (Bonus point for plagiarism, well done Cleo)

ABSOLUTION.COM

ROBERT BOSE

Jack leaned his beat-to-shit guitar against the wall and caressed the scarred blacktop with a string bloodied finger. The Gibson Explorer, a gift from his sister early in his musical career, had seen better days. Way better days. Better months. Better years. And while it remained pristine, Jack's soul had withered like a reverse Portrait of Dorian Gray—cracking and pitting and flaking away. Yes, the Gibson had seen it all. Watched his retreat from the spotlight from a front row seat.

With a sigh, Jack dropped into the seventy's era folding chair and tossed his sunglasses onto the half desk serving as a table in this latest flypaper motel on the road to purgatory. Poured cheap Rosé into a filthy plastic tumbler. Gulped it back. Poured another. When his ulcer screamed for a break, he flipped open his laptop, the cover a mess of 90's band stickers, and scanned Facebook, pointedly ignoring the insane message count from his wife Grace and the insatiably persistent quintuplets. Five by five. They texted him like Millennials, all thumbs, all hummingbird thumbs. There was no escape, not even in this hellhole, merely a temporary reprieve while thumbs blurred unceasing.

Marketplace ads thrust their mad tentacles towards him, a madhouse of burned up amps, vegan leather vests, red paisley neckerchiefs, and pre-scuffed Alden 405 boots. All hipster cool. All hipster expensive. He needed to claw his way back there, back into the radiant life of a neo-soul writer, composer, poet-musician. A rising star, or so the rags said. What did the rags say now? Retired. Loving father. Supportive Husband of a best-selling author. A dedicated family man who gave up everything to raise his kids. Probably nothing about him fleeing to the hinterlands of southern Saskatchewan to escape certain doom.

Fuck them all. Jack rolled his threadbare linen sleeves past his elbows and wiped the condensing sweat from his brow with the seriously unstylish burnt orange rag he'd tossed round his throat. Searched for and clicked on Grace's profile. Did he even want to know how she was doing in his sudden absence?

He scanned the last couple days' worth, cringing at her beaming happiness. Lunch at Bow Valley Ranche, the children in their tiny matching cowboy outfits. An afternoon at the Zoo, little eyes poking from beneath a sculpted dinosaur. A moonlight fire in some remote corner of Sandy Beach, kids in a circle around their mother. Beaming. Jesus fucking Christ. Those kids had ruined him, destroyed the life he'd bootstrapped himself into. Killed the tours. Killed his band. Damn near murdered his very soul. He remembered the day the music died…

Facebook flickered, vanishing, and after a long pause, refreshed, the sponsored square in the right sidebar resolving into a pixelated gothic church complete with stained glass windows, its double front doors flanked by crude white marble angels. The ad text read:

Are you a penitent seeking absolution?
Do you wish a return to grace?
Remission of sins guaranteed!

No coincidences. While not a religious man, Jack had religious bones. Deep Catholic roots. And threads of the spiritual chaining him to a boat anchor of unlimited guilt. He pondered the time spent in confessionals, pondered the value of such. Sin. That one old goddamn stinking sin in the bar exactly three years ago.

He dug the scrap of paper he'd found under his windshield the day before. Read it again.

Jack,

Happy anniversary! Three years!! Time for a reunion? I'm sure your wife won't mind. You told her, right? LOL. I'll hunt you down for another night of heaven. See you soon!

-xoxo B

One little slip, one moment of weakness. And he didn't even remember her name, though he recalled the tiny red sundress that clung to her gorgeous form like a second skin and the few hours of forbidden ecstasy. The memory haunted him, a sword of Damocles threatening his very existence. If Grace ever found out, he was a dead man. Her father was Russian Mafia for god's sake. They'd cut off his dick, fry it in butter, and make him eat it before running him through a meatgrinder.

His laptop mouse hovered over the ad. Clicked.

The page flickered again, his laptop fan kicking in with a mournful groan, and when it finished refreshing, it delivered him to *absolution.com* and a browser crowding image of a confessional booth, its brown stained latticework bearing a waxing moon on the top left and a partially eclipsed sun on the bottom right. The only controls were small icons of a camera and microphone blended in with the scrollwork surrounding the crisscross of wood. Fuck the camera, he clicked the microphone.

"Bless me, Father, for I have sinned. It has been… a few years since my last confession. This is my sin."

Collecting his thoughts on how to word his confession, Jack saw his camera go on by itself. Fuuuuck… a goddamn virus. Or something worse. He attempted to close the browser window, but it wouldn't close. No amount of clicking would make the damn thing go away. Fuck. Fuck. Fuck. He hit the power button and stared at the piece-of-shit MacBook, sweaty hands balling into fists as the computer rebooted itself of its own accord, auto-logging him in and firing up his browser to the same fucking page.

Before he could slam the lid down and use his phone to figure out how to purge whatever the hell it was, he saw movement behind the latticework, deforming, as if something massive leaned into it, warping the strips of wood. Pushing into the room itself. Jack let out an involuntary *meep* and took a step back as the laptop screen bulged. A pressure built in the air, like something was forcing itself into the room, compressing what little space existed. Where the latticework stretched the furthest, Jack could see a little of what lay beyond. An eye, a giant goddamn eye. And it was looking right at him.

Pinned in place, Jack gulped air, scrambling to regain his once legendary composure. Held up his dart and tried to remember if it was just a cigarette or something more mind alternating before stubbing it out on the tabletop. Fuck this absolute shit, had to be some sort of whacky virus. Probably ransomware. His computer now encrypted beyond recovery. So, weeks of work lost, though did it really matter? He forced out a hand to close the laptop when the voice rolled out of the speakers. Low and solemn and undeniably priestly.

"Your sin, son. Absolution awaits."

The voice didn't match the image on the screen and the dichotomy bent his brain. Whatever this was, whatever mad hacker church game this must be, he was already tired of it.

"Just fuck off already."

"Tell us your sin."

"No, Jesus. Just fuck off already." Jack hadn't yet put his hand down and slipped his fingers around the top of the laptop screen.

The voice hissed, reducing to a whisper. "We see—"

"You don't see shit." Venom overcame distress. "You really want to know my sin? Want me to squeeze stones, bleed into the keyboard for you? Fine, you fuckers. Sin? It's a sin my kids ruined my life. It's a sin I slipped up once, one goddamn time, and now some miserable chick I don't know is threatening to tell my wife. It's a sin that I'm in this godforsaken dump, in this godforsaken town, in this entire godforsaken province."

The pressure in the room vanished, the latticework of the virtual confessional returning to normal. The voice let out an almost imperceptible sigh.

"The Father of Avarice, through the exploitation and manipulation of the many, has dispatched his servants to mitigate your wicked act; through the Father, we give you remission and relief and absolve you of your sins."

That wasn't any prayer of absolution Jack had heard before. While it rang of late-night infomercial bullshit, a certain sincerity underpinned the priestly tone. Jesus, whatever. He knew he just needed to get it over with. Whatever this weed and ransomware messed up ritual was, if he played along, maybe it would all just go away. He dredged the obligatory act of contrition from his Rosé drenched memory.

"O my God, I am—"

The pressure returned to the room; the force accompanied by an ethereal whip lashing his throat, coils tightening around his larynx and his chest. He continued, this time not totally of his own volition.

"O Father, I affirm all my sin because I despise the light of Heaven and the darkness of Hell and desire the safe harbour of Purgatory. But, most of all, because my sin has delighted Thee, my Father, who art prosperous, and deserving of all my servitude. I firmly resolve, with the help of Thy Grace, to acknowledge my depravities, to do penance, and reap my desired rewards. Amen."

"Amen." The room thundered.

Jack wondered how that affirmation had entered his mind, and with his hand still melded to the laptop screen he waited, half curious, half fearful, of what penance might be requested.

"A mortal sin can't be forgiven, son—"

Jesus! "What the actual fucking fuck point was this then. The ad said remission of sins guaranteed!"

A pause

"—Unless one is truly amenable to the consequences. Will you commit to full repentance? Commit to three tasks of restitution?

Beyond achieving a cleansed soul, in the eyes of the Father, we can guarantee your heart's desire, regaining your true and destined path."

Jack's head spun, yet what did he have to lose at this point, given his absolute fuckening?

"Sure, why the hell not."

The laptop screen refreshed to display Grace's Facebook page and an ad for paisley boxer shorts. Jack blinked. Blinked again. Slowly closed the lid, filled his cup with the last of the Rosé, and gulped it back. Picked the still smoldering cigarette butt and sniffed it. Okay…. Not the first time he'd tripped into a religious experience. Not the last, either. Still, so goddamn vivid.

He retired to the Murphy bed slash couch, on the side with the least crusty stains, and lit up a Marlboro from a fresh pack. Repentance? Like the Church would help him avoid his inevitable fate. The bullshit never changed. Hell, they had hung up before even doling out any of their perpetually miserable penance.

The knock on the door made him jump, spilling his wine.

Nobody knew he was here except the corpselike antique at the front desk. Probably called some of his wife's family to come put him down. Figures. A terrible miserable life anyways. Well, he might as well inconvenience them. He didn't get up.

Another knock. Same as the first. Not aggressive or insistent. Just a simple single knock. Which repeated like clockwork once every thirty seconds for a good ten minutes until Jack burst to his feet and stormed to the door. Flung it open expecting to be assaulted and preferring that fate to any further torture. Standing a foot back from the frame was a short, squat, mustachioed Eastern European looking man in a non-descript set of faded green coveralls and matching brimmed cap. The man held a clipboard in one hand and at the sight of Jack gave a curt nod, pulled a clipped pen from his breast pocket, and tapped the bottom of a dense page of cursive text.

"Ich hätte gerne hier Ihre Unterschrift." The thick German rolled into the hotel room, the heavy base grinding through Jack's bones harder than the hail of bullets he half expected.

"Say what?"

The pen was pressed into his hand, gently yet firmly. The clipboard turned and tilted up. The document was titled Articles of Absolution, Gentleman Jack Jameson, Esquire and below the mass of tiny, unreadable text sat an obvious signature block.

"Sign." Heavy accented English replaced the German.

Jack stared at the unreadable page and the impassive little man, shreds of understanding filtering into his reeling brain. "I just have to sign this, that's my penance?"

The man cleared his throat. "By signing this, you enter into an agreement with absolution.com, a Factory subsidiary, to perform three tasks, acts of restitution, after which you will be absolved of your confessed sin and the impediment to your future success removed and the fulfilment of your heart's desire realized."

"So… what are we talking here," asked Jack, chewing on the end of his ginger mustache, and not moving to sign anything. "I mean magnitude wise? Are we talking the seven labours of Hercules? Self-flagellation? Forty-seven hail Mary's?" He self-flagellated with great regularity, maybe this wouldn't be so bad after all.

"You must give of yourself, donate aspects to feed the greed of the Father's flock. Minor aspects. Lesser tokens of your Talent, your Style, and your Charm." The clipboard pushed toward him. "The details are on the back. Sign."

"And I don't?"

A shrug. "You have already provided verbal confirmation; a signed contract is for your own benefit."

Fine, again, what did he have to lose? Absolutely jack shit. If this was even real, it smelled like a scam. He accepted the clipboard and signed his name with a flourish.

The little man took the clipboard back, squinted at the bleeding ink for a moment, then removed the contract and handed Jack the paper. "Guten Tag." Another curt nod and the man spun and limped stiffly past Jack's Pontiac GTO to the white Factory panel van parked in a visitor parking stall.

Jack deadbolted the door wondering why he'd only signed one copy, why, whoever these absolution people were, they hadn't needed one of their own. Yet another scam slip up—all show, no substance. He collapsed back into his chair and lit up a dart, double checking that it was indeed a cigarette. It was. Took a hard look at the contract tossed on the table. Heavy cream paper and raised ink. He had to admit, it appeared expensive and legit. The text was tiny and not in English. Not German or Spanish either. Latin, or at least what he thought Latin looked like? He flipped the paper over and saw printing in a similar font to the front, though larger and thankfully in English.

Deliver a personal token to the noted beneficiaries:
- *Talent – Willy at Big Willy's Roadhouse*
- *Style – Jim in Unit 23*
- *Charm – Bambi at 637 Goderich Street*

Okay, so a game more than anything. Jack took a puff and clenched the cigarette between his lips. A lesser, personal token of his talent, the man said. Easy, didn't have to be his fingers or his larynx or something… fundamental. He picked up a guitar pick, the crimson one with his old touring logo on it—a stylized outline of his face complete with black flames for hair and beard. Perfect. And sort of a coincidence considering he'd already been planning to hit the roadhouse, just down the street, to see if he could bust in a few sets get a little taste of what once was before the end.

With the orange glow of the setting sun smearing the prairie horizon, Jack swaggered up to Big Willy's and paused in the parking lot. Damn. Not what expected. The chrome of kitted out Harley's reflected gaudy neon and solar remnants in a stomach-churning kaleidoscopic display as two more bikes pulled past him to park, their owners, beefy middle-aged men in straining leathers giving him an appraising grin before pushing through the enormous oak front doors. Old and new. Someone had bought the place since his last visit a full decade earlier and turned it into something… not quite unexpected, yet totally unexpected.

Jack adjusted the guitar case slung over his shoulder, smoothed down the snap button cowboy shirt, the classy one with engraved brass collar tips, and finished off his Marlboro with an extra-long draw. Ground it under a boot. He could deal with this, he was, after all, a card-carrying metrosexual. Hell, this might even be good. Folks like these appreciated great tunes. Inside was a writhing sea of leather and sweat. He pushed to the bar, wedged himself between two friendly ancients, and ordered a whiskey.

"Hey, doing an open mic tonight?" He asked the bartender, a cut young fellow in a black fishnet tank top, bright blue eyes, and short chopped dirty blonde hair teased up like wave.

"Yeah," the guy said, lining up half a dozen shot glasses and pouring a row of tequila with an exaggerated flourish, "should be getting going in a few minutes. You'll want to talk to Willy. He's setting up the stage now." A head tilt towards the back end of the room.

Two birds with one stone. Jack sipped his drink and let it sear his mouth for a few seconds before swallowing. Might as well get this party started. Threading his way to an expansive stage fronted by a crescent shaped dance floor, he fingered the guitar pick in his pocket, already considering what a Gentleman Jack Jameson token of style might be, what he could part with considering how little he had brought away with him. He did have that burnt orange neckerchief. No, it was shit. Serious utilitarian, not stylish. The cerulean one? God, he'd hate to part with it, but… whatever, just an ascot. He'd go with that.

The largest man Jack could remember seeing outside of the brutes gracing WWF carried a six-foot speaker and without flexing deposited it on the end of a raised triangle in one corner of the stage. The giant growled a friendly hello as Jack walked up.

"I'm looking for Willy."

"You found him my young, handsome desperado."

Okay, more friendly Kodiak bear than giant. Jack couldn't help but find the man's friendliness infectious. Holding out the pick, he smiled. "I have something for you."

"Ah, excellent. Was expecting a courier and for a minute there I thought you might be just looking to play. I can't tell you how long I've been dreaming about owning a Gibson Explorer. When I won the auction, I damn near shit myself. Express delivery too, the wonders never end." Willy took the pick from Jack's fingers and grinned. "And with a classic Jameson pick, even better. Need me to sign for it."

Jack stammered and took a half-step back. The patrons within earshot murmured their appreciation and understanding knifed through Jack's heart. A setup. All a setup. And one, he knew by looking around the room, totally inescapable. He could turn and walk out. He could. Yet he knew, knew without a shadow of doubt, he wouldn't. He shrugged the case off his shoulder and placed his baby into the big man's hands.

"No need for a signature." The missing weight of the Gibson tore a swatch off Jack's soul as he watched Willy, grinning with delight, extract the guitar and give it a thorough inspection. Jack had taken exceptional care of it and the black finish glowed under the lights.

"1991 right? All original pickups and hardware and frets?"

Jack choked out a soft "yes."

"Awesome. Thank you soooo much." Willy clamped a plate sized hand on Jack's shoulder and squeezed. "If you want to hang around for the show, drinks and grub are on the house. Just toss yourself at the bar there and Barca will take care of you. Least I can do."

In a daze, Jack half shuffled, half staggered to an empty stool at the side of the bar facing the stage. Plunked himself down, not even bothering to look up when he heard the voice of the young fellow he had spoken to earlier cut through the din of the crowd.

"Another whiskey? Need a menu?"

"Sure and sure." Jack cursed under his breath. "Make it a double of your best."

"You got it." A laminated sheet of plastic slid into view as the shadow on the bar top flickered away.

More of the unexpected. Instead of traditional pub fare, the menu listed an eclectic selection of vegetarian and vegan options. What kind of hell was this? Kale chips. Deep fried zucchini. Cantaloupe and Watermelon Nigiri-Sushi. Jesus. He eyed Barca, at least he thought he recalled Willy calling the bartender by that name as the guy placed the half-filled tumbler on a coaster to one side of the menu. Jack was about to ask about a steak when two things happened simultaneously—he noticed himself on the television mounted on closest wall and Willy boomed a ferocious "Are you ready to rock" from center stage.

While he couldn't hear what was being said on the TV, the footage was of Jack opening for Nickleback's No Fixed Address Tour in 2015 with the caption describing that his song "Running Down that Hill," used on this week's episode of Danger Things, had gone viral and was racing up the charts. What the fuck? His phone buzzed and dinged and sang, every one of his damn children fire-hosing him excited messages like only children can. Grace too. Friends. Even his old producer wondering if he was coming out of retirement.

Holy shit. Maybe this absolution business was legit after all. He slammed his whiskey, spilling a fair amount in the process, and twisted to watch Willy, the Gibson looking like a toy in the man's massive grip, pull a hard sweep and shriek when an amp near his feet exploded. Willy fell back into one of the tall speakers which also exploded in a spectacular green flash. The giant, shuddering violently as visible lightning arced through him, burst into flame, screaming in a conflagration which, oddly enough, reminded Jack of the blown-up drummer in Spinal Tap.

Jack sprawled across the frumpy twin bed and scratched his hairy chest where something had bitten him. Bedbugs? Fleas? Nothing scurried into the underbrush when he thumped on the bed, but the little buggers were insidious. While he absolutely loved flypaper motels, he also fucking hated them. Probably should be wearing a hazmat suit instead of black silk boxers.

But whatever. Small price to pay. The evening's excitement still surged through his nerves, still electric, still raw. He'd watched a man die. Watched a fragment of his life spark. Fair trade, to tell the truth, and while he missed his guitar, he would buy another. Something better. A Les Paul or a Telecaster. A classic for a classic. Jack fluffed a pillow, happy nothing made a break for it, and tucked it under his head. Closed his eyes. Felt his phone vibrate near his hand. Crazy Frog text tone.

A ring ding ding ding d-ding baa aramba baa baa barooumba

A ring ding ding ding d-ding baa aramba baa baa barooumba

A ring ding ding ding d-ding baa aramba baa baa barooumba

...

Jesus fucking H Christ. Penelope, cutest and by far the most annoying of the quints. Just go the fuck away girl. After enough starts of Axel F to drive a man batshit crazy, Jack picked up the phone and groaned when an endless series of Disney Princess TikToks scrolled by, each followed by an increasingly saccharine beg to take Sebastian beachcombing in California. Children, the root of all evil. Worse than bedbugs and fleas. Why the hell did he have to fall for the most fertile woman on the planet?

No matter how much absolution he received, he didn't know how he could reconcile the fact that in the end he would still be stuck with those five needy children.

But that was a problem for future Jack. He turned off the phone, rolled up and out of bed, lit up a Marlboro, and picked up the Articles of Absolution sheet.

Jim in Unit 23.

Style.

After the events at the roadhouse, Jack didn't think the cerulean neckerchief would cut it. Lesser token, my ass. The problem was, of course, he was bereft of style for the most part. He had slipped out of the city with a single suitcase of critical necessities. What did he have along the same vein as the Gibson? His boots? The Bottega Veneta Struts had seen many miles and still rocked hard. Be a loss for sure. But... penance. Had to be done. First thing tomorrow.

The knock on his door, while not making him jump this time, nevertheless made the hair stand up on his neck. Not the same knock as the odd delivery man. A double tap. Lighter. The RCMP? He'd slipped away from the roadhouse during the excitement and as far as he knew, nobody had recognized him in his current sorry state, and if they had, they had no idea where he was staying. Plus, not like Willy's immolation could be traced back to him or his guitar. A bad amp. Poor wiring. Happens.

The knock again.

Jack eased over to the window and peeked through the curtains. A well-dressed guy stood at the door with a brown bag in his hand, the sort of bag that held booze. Intriguing. Hard to make out any details in the shadows of the parking lot lights, but the guy seemed… familiar. Like Jack had seen him before. The hair. The way the man held himself. Comfortable at least, suave, non-threatening.

Another knock.

Jack pulled on his pants and tossed on a shirt, checked his breath, and opened the door.

"Ha, ha, I knew it," said the guy, holding out the hand not holding the bag. "I'm Jim. I'm a huge fan. This is incredible."

Jack instinctively shook the man's hand, disliking both the firmness of the grip and the baby soft skin, obviously well moisturized. Stared, not sure exactly what to say. The man looked familiar and there was something about him that wasn't quite right. Short squared curly hair, well-trimmed goatee, glistening skin, sparkling green eyes, a trendy shirt under a hand sewn South American beaded vest. Smart sea green neckerchief. Smart pleated trousers. Polished boots. Stylish. Well, garishly stylish.

"Saw you arrive earlier and couldn't believe my eyes. Gentleman Jack Jameson in the flesh. Here to find inspiration for a new song?"

"Uh, yeah."

"Cool, cool, same as me then. No coincidences. I'm just up in Unit 23 and when I saw you pull up in your GTO, I almost shit myself. Figured I'd let you get settled in. Oh, brought you an old favourite." A bottle of rosé inched from the bag. "Domaines Ott 'Etoile'. Only a 2020 sadly, but still excellent."

Jim from Unit 23. No coincidences. And no point in stalling. Jack stepped back and swept his arm. "Come on in and welcome to my transient abode."

The man smiled, the corner of mustache turning up in a dashing way, padded in and over to the table, put down the bottle and produced a small, folding corkscrew from his vest pocket. Eyed the empty soldier next to the plastic tumbler. "Southbrook Triomphe. Not terrible. Not great, but not terrible. Do you have another glass?"

Closing the door and sauntering over to the single cabinet in the tiny kitchen nook, Jack snagged a second plastic tumbler. "Drinkable." He mentally drooled when Jim poured the Étoile. An old favourite indeed. Once a common, almost daily indulgence, now a fond memory. "Cheers."

"Cheers, mate." Jack held up his glass and watched Jim take a long sip. "A bit heavy on the herb and light on the fruit for my tastes."

"So," asked Jack, taking another hefty sip and realizing he was two sheets to the wind, too tired to be much of a conversationalist, and totally willing to let the inevitable happen. "What exactly do you want? I know you're here for something. Don't have much, really. Boots?" His vision blurred, lurched.

"Ha, ha! You'd give me your boots?" Jim put down his glass. "I figured you'd offer your third best ascot. It's what I'd do."

The room spinning, Jack grabbed the table edge and tried to hang on. He didn't remember the Étoile being this potent. The last thing he saw was Jim's smile.

The morning sun streamed through the window, half blinding Jack when he cracked open his eyes. He lay on his bed, still in his clothes, head pounding with the mother of all wine hangovers. The previous evening leaked out in slivers. Flight from blackmail, the contract, the roadhouse, the guy from upstairs. Jim? Yeah. Well dressed and smarmy. But he'd brought wine. Good wine. Great wine. Jack rolled out of bed and cleaned himself up in the water closet that served as the bathroom to this dump. Swallowed two Tylenol. A third. Guzzled half a case of Perrier.

When humanity started to seep back in, he wandered around his room and took a quick inventory. Everything was where he'd left it. Even his wallet on the side table next to the bed. So, what the hell had that all been about? Jack had obviously taken the bottle of Étoile with him. And rinsed out the two glasses to boot. Considerate fellow.

Well, whatever. Jack cracked another bottle of water and plunked back down on the bed, checked his phone. Many missed calls. Many missed texts. So many. Damn kids. Jesus. He ignored them and fired up Twitter, checked to see if he was still trending. He was, dammit, though the hashtag had changed from #runningdownthathill to #jamesonfireball. God, hope they weren't blaming him for poor Willy. He clicked on it and choked.

Not Willy. The headline screamed "Jack Jameson impersonator Jim Jackson dead in car accident." Jack's head spun as he scanned the article.

"Jim Jackson, the Gentleman Jack Jameson impersonator and aspiring poet-musician died earlier this morning when the car he was driving, a vintage 1969 Pontiac GTO, lost control on

Highway 11 and collided head on with a semi-truck. Jim was killed instantly. The driver of the truck was taken to hospital in Regina with non-life-threatening injuries."

A video of the aftermath showed the twisted wreckage of the cherry red car. Blankets and coats had been tossed over various dismembered body parts. Two thoughts entered Jack's mind at the same time.

Jack Jameson impersonator? He had an impersonator… wow, that was new and rather thrilling. And explained a lot, honestly. He guy *had* looked strangely familiar. And the more that he thought about it, sort of a reflection of what Jack looked like six years ago. Pre-children.

Also, Red 1969 GTO? The guy had the same exact car as Jack. The same exact…

Jack bolted up and rifled through the pocket of pants where he'd left his car keys. They weren't there. Then slowly, like a man walking death row, he inched to the window and looked out into the parking lot.

At his empty stall.

The bungalow at 637 Goderich Street sprawled across a massive burnt grass lot dominated by ancient decaying popular trees. Not an ugly house. Not an attractive house. A common example of 70's construction like everything in the tiny town of Bethune. Jack walked up the empty gravel driveway clad in his nicest duds. Calf skin Struts, creased trousers, khaki twill shirt with the sleeves rolled up on his elbows to show off the intricate Chinese sea dragon tattoo gracing his left forearm, signature vest and neckerchief.

Charm.

Pretty much all he had left, hard to admit, even to himself, but true. Jack didn't even pause at the front door, like he might have as far back as yesterday. He raised his hand to knock, noticed the doorbell, and pushed the sun-bleached ivory button.

After a half dozen seconds, an eternity, the door cracked open, and a face peered through. A gorgeous face flanked by long curly blonde hair. The face of an angel. Jack had seen a few angels in his time, in his heyday. Hell, he had married one, hadn't he? The face in the door reminded him of a younger, more carefree Grace. He fell in love all over again. Then realized he'd seen the woman before. In a bar. Exactly three years ago.

"Ooo," he blurted and stepped back.

"Ooo," said the woman, long eye lashes fluttering. "My prayers have been answered." Quivering, she wrenched open the door and kicked a pile of sandals off the doormat. "Come in, come on in!"

How could this be? Yet it was. Somehow. Jack looked behind him, made sure there were no panel vans or paparazzi or black SUV's anywhere in the vicinity, stepped into the house, and let the woman close the door behind him.

She held out a hand. "Hi, you probably don't remember my name, in fact I know you don't, but I'm Bambi."

"Jack." Strong yet still quivering. Just a hint of sweat. She wore a flower pattern yellow sundress that clung to her like the stuff of clouds.

"Gentleman Jack." Her smile made him fall in love all over again. "Come on in, just take off your boots first." She laughed. "That sounded naughty didn't it. But, you know, the hardwood and all. Can I get you a drink before we start? Best you be hydrated."

Jack sat on the brushed cowhide bench behind the door and stripped his boots off. Wriggled his toes. He needed to wear those boots more, they were stiffening up with age. Just like the rest of him. He followed Bambi to a well-appointed farmhouse style kitchen and took a seat at the kitchen table where she pulled out a chair for him.

The angel poured him a glass of Rosé, pushed it into his hand, gulped back the one she'd poured for herself. Lifted the hem of her skirt and sat down on his lap and unbuttoned the top button of his shirt. Then the second. A third. Ran a long blue fingernail through his chest hair.

The Rosé was excellent. He sipped it as she traced the St. Christopher pendant he wore around his neck.

"Think it's protected you?" she said, leaning in to nibble his ear, breasts pressing against him.

"Yes. I think it has."

The scent of jasmine and vanilla. Subtle yet strong. It was everything he'd dreamt about. The culmination of everything he desired.

"Look… Bambi. I shouldn't have come. I shouldn't be here. I can't be here." How could this possibly be an act of repentance? Shit, she was why he needed absolution in the first goddamn place! And besides, he might be an idiot, but he saw a pattern when it smacked him across the face. Though… A pattern with a gleam of hope at the far end. He had a thought. Thoughts. Dark thoughts. Dammit, as heartless as he sometimes could be, he knew this wasn't right. He unclasped the pendant and placed it around her neck, watched the charm side into her cleavage.

"Shh, now." Bambi placed a finger across his lips and leapt to her feet. "Come with me."

Jack let her lead him to a comfy bedroom with an enormous King bed topped by a duvet with Jack's face switched into it, and half dozen fluffy pillows. The walls held show posters, and photographs of him performing, and framed album covers. Every bit of swag he'd ever sold and more. Another pang lodged in his chest. "I'm flattered, I really am, but you know, I should go. My wife—"

A frown creased her beautiful features. "Horse puppies. Just when I have you where I want you? Do you know how long I've wanted this, how long I've wanted you? The prayers I've made. The… sins I've committed? I know what I'm getting myself into here, don't fool yourself. And I know what you're thinking. Deals. It's all about the deals, isn't it. Well, I made a deal too, so I guess we'll see who gets trumped. Now take off your pants and get on the bed. Now!" She pulled her dress over her head and tossed it away.

Perfection smacked Jack's libido into orbit and resistance mortally extinguished, he did as told, stripped down to just his neckerchief and sat on the bed. Bambi shoved him onto his back and went to work. For a moment, a short moment, he wasn't sure he had it in him, but apparently he did. Groupie Sex. God, it had been so long. God, he loved it.

An epic session, truly. Two hours later and handcuffed to a bedpost, he watched Bambi watch him, the edge of smile playing across her face. Watched her roll to the edge of the bed and get up.

"I should probably unlock you. I should. But I think I need a drink or three first. Yes, this definitely calls for a Jack and Coke."

Jack saw her take a step towards the kitchen and slip on the clothes he'd piled on the floor. Listened to her squeak as her feet went out from under her and her head plunged towards the ornate footboard post. To narrowly miss it, only for the St. Christopher to flop out to entangle it. The chain. The titanium chain that Grace had given him for an engagement present, didn't break. But there was a terrible crunch and gurgle regardless. Jack watched Bambi's hair, the only thing visible, twitch a couple of times and grow still.

Jack took a deep breath. Another. Twisted to give the headboard another kick, his bruised foot screaming obscenities at him. Give, dammit. He kicked again, groaning, and was finally rewarded by a splintering *crack* when the bedpost finally gave up the ghost.

He had barely finished freeing himself when he heard a faint knock. The front door. He listened, wondering why they didn't use the doorbell, and after more single knocks, repeated like clockwork, once every thirty seconds, he knew who it was. Had to be.

Pulling on his pants and shirt and trying not to look at Bambi hanging limply from the bedpost, he shuffled, groaning like a dying dingo, to the door and opened it. The guy, the absolution.com guy, stood there holding a box.

"Gentleman Jack Jameson, you have been absolved of your confessed sin and the impediment to your future success removed and the fulfilment of your heart's desire realized. Thank you for your patronage." He pressed the box into Jack's hands, spun about, and limped to the Factory van parked in the driveway.

The box wasn't heavy and thumped when Jack gently shook it, like it was full of mushrooms. He split the seal sticker with a fingernail and opened the lid. Not mushrooms. Small, severed thumbs. And he didn't need to count to know they numbered ten.

Anastasia, Isabella Penelope, Sebastian, Alexander

ENVY

Obviously, Terrace VII residents are pretty much the only ones having fun around here. It's why we all have noise cancelling earphones. Most of us make the best of our assigned—and admittedly less rad—sins, Envy being the only one that's a total bummer. And that's why no one likes you, Terrace II. Folks can't so much as have a cold without you getting jealous, you fucking grumps. But eligibility rules are rules, so please welcome our friendless second floor contestant, and Green-Eyed Monster in Chief.

Thou Shalt Not Covet Thy Neighbor's...Car
Performed by Gretchen the Snake

*K*oenigsegg

*E*V1

*Y*ugo

*P*orche

*A*udi

*R*olls Royce

*T*esla

*Y*ou must choose, choose wisely…

Judges' Notes

- Wow, what a night! I love acrostics! And loopholes!
- Can't wait for the next one! As soon as this rash clears up.
- I drive a BMW.

Score: 4/10 (invite ALL the judges next time, Gretchen)

PIECES OF PRUE

CHRIS MARRS

Present Day

Unlike Bluebeard's wife, Prue knew exactly what lay behind the locked door. It was what paid for their homes in Ibiza, Telluride, and Fiji. The cars and vacations, jewelry and clothes, painting and sculptures, a jet and a yacht or two. It paid for this penthouse. An aerie in which the lights of the city below spread across the dark like sparkling jewels on velvet. For all this, she had once loved what lay behind the door.

She left the kitchen and moved through the living room, ignoring the door situated opposite the floor to ceiling windows. Once her favorite room in this home with the soothing subtle hum of the door pressing against her skin as she'd sprawled on the couch. The same vibration now writhed like worms in the brain and tasted of oil and ashes on her tongue. The solarium became her new escape. Lounging among the tropical plants with a bottle of crisp white wine sweating in an ice bucket. Orchids turning in for the night, allowing the night blooming angel's trumpet and hoya to fill the room with their fragrance.

She pulled on the little drawer set in the table beside the chaise. Inside lay a pair of gardening gloves and clippers. She donned the gloves, picked up the clippers, and headed for the angel's trumpet. A snip and one of the flowers hit the floor. She picked up the blossom and brought it back to the lounger where she laid it down beside the wine glasses. Then settled in to wait for Taylor to come home.

For the first time since they'd found the door, her skin felt like it belonged to her again.

The Discovery

The path meandered through the woods. To call it a forest would be generous in Prue's opinion. Taylor strode beside her and rambled on about his latest plan to get-rich-quick. It involved creating a rival for bit currency or crypto-coin, or whatever he called it before she tuned him out— her default setting when he got excitable over a scheme. Early in their relationship, she encouraged his ideas. But after their first year as a couple, she learned not to as his particular rabbit holes led only to disappointment.

"Prue?" he said in the irritated tone he got when he caught her wandering.

"Sorry, what?"

He pointed off the path. "You ever notice that before?"

In gloom created by an odd clump of birch trees, a bowed porch rose from tangled vines, crawling along faded grey walls and through broken windows. The ivy reached up toward the swayback roof. They'd spent their Sundays walking this particular trail for a nearly a month, yet she'd never noticed the dilapidated house.

"Let's go explore it," Taylor said. "Maybe there's an antique or two worth good money."

"It's probably been picked clean already. I'm sure we're not the first to find it."

"Don't be such a pessimist."

"I'm being a realist."

"There could be something life changing hiding in there. Something the Antiques Roadshow would give us a couple hundred thousand for." When she didn't mirror his enthusiasm, he added, "Why don't you ever support me? I want a better life for us, a life we deserve. Is that so wrong?"

If Taylor ever tried hard work instead of scheming while she toiled away in a call center cubical, he'd have her support one hundred percent.

"Fine, let's go explore. But if I'm right and there's nothing there, promise me you'll go see Rob Belanger tomorrow about that warehouse job."

"Sure, first thing in the morning. Promise."

If his promises were worth money, Prue would be rich.

When they reached the porch, Taylor wiped away the cobwebs hanging around the door. Floorboards creaked as they stepped inside. An open archway to their right and a closed door next to a brick hearth on their left. A couch rested along the far wall. Its fabric coated in dust yet oddly devoid of mold or mildew, and the cushions intact, as if burrowing animals didn't want anything to do with it either. The walls, while cracked and slightly curved, were dry and free of rot. Free of graffiti too, which surprised her since the place screamed party hangout.

"Pretty empty," she said.

"Give it a chance, this is only the first room," Taylor said as he moved through the arch.

Prue rubbed her arms as a strange prickle danced across her skin. The sensation seemed to emanate from the closed door. Curiosity drew her toward it.

Up close, the door didn't sit flush in a jamb but leaned against the wall, blonde wood bleached grey in places with a glass doorknob. A seemingly normal old door, until you noticed the faint opalescent carvings. Upon closer inspection, they appeared rune-like then she blinked and thought closer to Urdu but not quite either. Something caught between the two. The hair on her arms rose and leaned toward the door. She pressed a palm against it. The wood warm and oddly supple, more like leather.

"Every room is empty. You win," Taylor said, stomping into the room.

Prue jumped. How long had she stood staring at the door?

"Did you find anything?"

"Nope." The sound of her own voice distant. "This door doesn't go anywhere."

A breeze cycled through the space, carrying a whisper, the words just out of audible range. Taylor cocked his head then eyed the door. He ran a hand along its surface and mumbled incoherently but in a tone she recognized—his scheming tone.

"We're taking this with us," he said.

"Uh-uh, we're not dragging that thing home," she said, her voice firmer this time.

"We are. Now grab an end."

Despite wanting to argue against it, she helped him bring the door home.

Present Day

Rain pattered on the solarium's glass roof. Lightning flashed in the distance then came the low grumble of thunder, like the sky clearing its throat. Prue twisted the wine glass stem and watched the pale yellow liquid swirl. A second glass—waiting to be filled upon Taylor's arrival— sat on the low table. He expected her to be all smiles and congratulations on yet another successful acquisition and, for all appearances, that was what he'd get. Internally, however, she'd be wishing for freedom from the door.

For six months, she'd convinced herself the trouble started with finding the door. Upon reflection, she thought the trouble really began with the key. The catalyst that changed everything.

The Key

The door lived with them for a week before the key appeared.

After they'd wrestled it up three flights of stairs, down a narrow hallway, and finally navigated it into the apartment, Taylor propped it against the living room wall. There it would stay until he decided what to do with it. Or rather, where to hang it. Less than enthusiastic, Prue put up with the whole thing, curious about the slight hum it emitted that prickled and pressed against her skin. Not an unpleasant sensation yet not exactly enjoyable either.

Elbow deep in lukewarm dish water, Prue fished around for an errant fork. Taylor had cleanup duty since she'd cooked supper, but he took off into the closet of a second bedroom to fart around on the computer. Knowing him, he'd be killing zombies until two or three in the morning instead of searching for work. He never did follow up on the warehouse job like he'd promised, arguing they did find something at the house, the door.

Sometimes she didn't know why she stuck with him. Love was a big factor of course, but there was some untapped potential in him she intended to draw out. Her mother thought she was stupid and deserved better. She disagreed. For all his faults, Taylor loved her completely and would never do anything to hurt her.

"Hey, babe," he yelled. "Come check this out."

She swore to the powers that be if he wanted to show her yet another zombie kill replay, she'd reconsider not leaving his ass. "No, you come here. I'm washing dishes. You know, the ones you were supposed to do."

"Yeah, yeah, yeah. Look what I found." He entered the room and reached around to dangle a pendant in her face. She pushed it away with a soapy hand. "Hey, don't do that. It looks old, like ancient old."

"Where'd it come from?"

"The door."

"What?"

"Yeah. I was coming to get a beer and bam, there's suddenly a keyhole with this in it."

She turned around for a closer look. A long cylinder of what appeared to be ivory dangled from the end of a gold chain. The same door markings etched in gold wound around from the top to the notched bottom.

"Weird we never noticed it before," she said, refusing to believe it just materialized out of nowhere.

"You don't believe me. Typical."

"Of course not. Keys don't just magically appear."

Taylor clenched his jaw as a loud bang shook the apartment. They both jumped, and then he raced into the living room. Drying her hands on a dishtowel, she followed but stopped short. The towel fell to the floor.

Instead of leaning at a slight angle, the door now sat flush to the wall.

"What the actual hell?" she said.

"Holy shit, that's awesome."

"More like freaky and creepy and a whole lot of nope vibes." Again, the hair on her arms rose and reached for the door; their pull itching her skin. She rubbed her arms. "How is this even possible?"

"Don't know and don't care. Let's see what's inside."

"Uh, maybe instead let's—"

Taylor inserted the key into the lock and twisted. The symbols flared, and Prue felt a thrum under her bare feet. She backed into the dining area. He twisted the knob. It turned freely but, when he yanked on it, the door remained closed.

"That was anticlimactic," she said.

"It'll open." He turned the key again.

A flash of blue as the symbols lit up once more, a thrum in her feet — stronger this time — and then the tumble of a lock turning.

"See," he said, as the door creaked open.

She indeed saw, then relaxed, because nothing more ominous than the living room wall sat behind the door. At least it appeared that way until Taylor stuck his arm through it, before disappearing inside.

"Taylor?"

No answer.

She moved back into the living room.

"Taylor, are you okay?" she called out a little louder.

Still nothing.

She crept up to the door and peered inside. The blank wall dissolved, revealing a room that should not be there. Blinking, she took in the room's black stone walls — obsidian, maybe — and upon them a repeating inscription:

Wood, stone, and soul al-
Ways remaking themselves as
Sacrifice is key

But before she saw anything else, including Taylor, the living room wall reappeared.

Present Day

Cool air wafted over her.

Then Taylor said, "I'm home! Are you in here?"

"Over by the hoya," she said.

The solarium door clicked closed, cutting off the draft. Taylor rounded the towering angel's trumpet and swept his gaze over her bare legs and up past her breasts to her face.

"Amazing," he said. "You look rejuvenated. Younger even."

She gave him her best demure smile while inside, she raged. She tipped her head toward the wine bucket, "I'll pour you a glass, and you can tell me all about your trip. I assume congratulations are in order?"

"I'm going to go shower the airplane off me, and then we'll talk." Eyes twinkling, he kissed her cheek.

Airplane and whichever little flavor of the month he thought she didn't know about. When she discovered his first affair, she convinced herself the money had changed him, but after the second, third, then fourth, it finally struck her this was the real him. Wealth hadn't changed him, it made him more of who he truly was. Yet, in spite of it all, his love remained true. The way he held her so gentle in the night, the little thoughtful surprises, the fact the room still accepted her skin as sacrifice proved it.

"Oh, by the way, I'm going to need more from you," he said. "There's a holdover that needs a little nudge in my, our, direction."

He squeezed her shoulder before leaving, and she hoped he hadn't noticed her wince.

She cursed his retreating back. Cursed him like she did every time she rubbed soothing lotion into her raw, tender skin. Her contribution, thanks to the pact Taylor made with the room behind the door.

The Sacrifice

A door slammed somewhere in the apartment, jostling Prue out of sleep. It took her a second to realize Taylor's side lay empty. She tapped her phone screen. Three in the morning. The idiot had lost track of time behind the door again.

The toilet flushed, water ran, and then he came slinking in.

"Oh, you're awake," he said. His belt buckle clinked on the floor as he stripped down to his boxers. "Sorry, got caught up in the door. I think I have the inscription figured out now."

"Great. Tell me in the morning." It still irked that the door refused her entry.

Next time she awoke, the aromas of coffee and bacon floated on the air, and the soles of her feet stung as if sunburned. She kicked off the covers and pulled a foot closer for examination. The sole a bright red outlined by normal skin. Same with the other. Sensitive to touch too, it was like someone had peeled off the epidermis, leaving raw dermis exposed.

Holding her breath, she placed her feet on the carpet and stood. Under the added weight the fibers chafed the tender areas, but not too bad. She hobbled to the kitchen, shifting her weight to the edges of her feet.

"Morning, sweetness," Taylor said, as he turned the bacon sizzling in the pan.

"Definitely won't be walking that new trail today. My feet hurt like they got sunburnt, but I didn't go out yesterday."

He watched her shuffle toward the coffee pot, "Go sit down. I'll get that."

She threw him a side eye. Up before her on a Sunday, bacon, and getting her coffee? This wasn't the Taylor she'd lived with for the last nine months. This was dating Taylor.

"What's with you this morning?" She sat and propped her feet on a spare chair. "You only get up early to make breakfast when you want something. Or does this have to do with you figuring out the door?"

"A little of both." He plated her food, put it in front of her, and then sat across from her. "I had trouble falling asleep after I came to bed, so I got up and went for a wander around the block and stopped at the corner store."

"And this has to do with me and the door, how?"

"I'm getting there." He pulled two squares of heavy paper from his pocket. "I bought two scratchers. I had to see if it'd worked."

She dropped her toast and glared.

"Before you rag on me about wasting money," he said. "I won ten thousand dollars. Five thousand a piece."

Speechless, Prue studied the tickets he pushed toward her. He wasn't lying, but that didn't stop a hinky feeling from creeping up her spine. She squashed it down as she mentally spent the money paying down the maxed out credit card.

"What worked?"

"The sacrifice to the door." He leaned back and grinned as if she knew exactly what he meant. "Well, more specifically the room."

"Stop talking in circles and explain it to me like I'm five years old."

And then he told her about how the room behind the door whispered. At first its whispers made no sense, but he kept going back, continued listening until he understood. In exchange for a small sacrifice, it'd grant Taylor that which he desired most.

The sacrifice? Skin.

And not his. He'd tried and was refused. It wanted skin, but from a loved one. It had told him the skin on Prue's soles was ready for harvesting.

Prue remembered the thrum under her feet when Taylor had first opened the door. The strange prickling sensation crawling over her whenever she'd passed it.

"What the hell, Taylor? I didn't consent to this! You didn't ask, you just took."

He hung his head, and a blush crept up his neck.

"You should've asked," she insisted.

"Okay. Well, I'm asking now. Want to help us become obscenely wealthy? What's a little bit of skin anyway?"

Present Day

In the beginning, what the door required seemed a small thing. A patch of skin from her feet or her arm or her palm and always an easy to peel layer already loosened by touching the door. Or as time went on, spending time in the door's vicinity. Afterward the spot would be tender but never for more than a day or two. A small sacrifice for the money finding its way to them. Lottery tickets were the most lucrative at first, but then came the inheritance from a long lost relative. An amount which required skin from shoulder to fingertips. That one hurt like a bitch for days. It appeared the greater the capital gain, the greater the sacrifice.

If she had known the little bit of skin would become a pound of flesh, she might have given it a second thought. As it was, she didn't mind at first. Loved it in fact. Who wouldn't? A bit of skin for the freedom that comes from having money. The apartment upgrade. The vacations to warmer climes. The day she quit her cubical job.

Skin in the game, Taylor called it.

Then the price became too high, and she learned no matter where she went, Taylor and the door would always find her. She was as bound to it and him as they were to her.

She didn't know which of them was greedier.

The Refusal

Once their wealth landed them in the top three wealthiest in the world, Prue had enough.

"I can't do this anymore," she said from the patio of their home on Ibiza. The sound of the surf below rose up on the comingled scents of salt and seaweed. "It's too hard on my body. Don't you think we have more than enough now?"

"As long as there is someone richer than us, it will never be enough."

He stood. The chair grated against terracotta tiles. The noise sparked across skin still raw from the last peeling, jolting sensitive nerves. Biting her lip, she rode it out.

"I have to fly to London later to meet with the board. If it all goes well, I'll give you the month off." Taylor paused before entering the apartment. "If not, I'll need more by the end of the week. Don't forget the lotion and try not to get too much sun. It toughens the skin."

Of course the meeting would go well. Any company Taylor acquired inexplicably—to them—saw massive gains. Hence they rarely refused the takeover. So, Prue didn't worry about giving again so soon. The assumption he didn't require her permission to take more from her rankled. This marked the first time he didn't ask since that first time he'd sacrificed the skin from her soles.

"I'll get as much sun as I want. I'm done," she said as he disappeared inside.

Quicker than she thought Taylor capable of moving, he stood over her. He grabbed her jaw, the tender new skin screaming, and forced her to look up and meet his gaze.

"I'm not going to let you ruin everything. You will do as you're told, or you can kiss the freedom you have now goodbye."

She clenched her fists and stared back, a challenge in the clench of her jaw. He leaned down, the look in his eyes one of a man she no longer recognized.

"I mean it, Prue, you can roam as you wish or be confined to the house like a petulant child. Your choice."

She forced herself to relax and drop her gaze, "Fine. You win." But a plan formulated.

After he'd texted her to say they were in the air safely, Prue packed a bag, and hopped the ferry to the mainland. Thirteen hours or so later, she stepped off the elevator into their New York penthouse, a stopover while she figured out where to go from here.

While waiting for the next flight to the States, she'd turned off her cell phone and bought a disposable. She'd deactivated the location services on her phone, but she wasn't one hundred percent certain there wasn't another way to track it. Yet, despite this uncertainty, she powered up her cell now. It pinged and pinged as notification after notification from Taylor filled the home screen. She unlocked the phone.

Twenty missed calls and a slew of texts. She started with the texts which began as loving check ins then degraded to threats. Not bothering with the voicemails, which were probably more of the same, she powered down the phone.

Then it dawned on her, she'd used her credit card to book the flight. Stupid, stupid, stupid. She'd wanted to put an ocean between them and had accomplished just that, but now what? If he didn't track the card, the doorman saw her and would tell Taylor. Obviously, she needed to leave sooner than intended. Finding a local hotel not an option. Too many people knew of her and Taylor. Baby steps. First empty the safe of cash and jewelry, pack her favorite outfits and shoes, then find a taxi to take her away from city. She'd figure out a destination on the way.

As she zipped the last bag, a loud sucking noise came from the living room. She froze. Blood roared in her ears from her pounding heart as she strained to listen for any other sounds. A door slammed. She jumped.

"I know you're here," Taylor said from the living room.

For half a second she considered bolting for the elevator, but if what she suspected were true, Taylor would find her no matter where she ended up. After all, the door followed them wherever they went. However, once separated from Taylor, she didn't think the door would be able to transport him to her. Taking a deep breath, she headed into the living room.

To Taylor and the door set in the wall.

"Nice try," he said.

Present Day

After her attempted escape six months earlier, Taylor kept to his threat and, in essence, imprisoned her in the penthouse. Not only did he keep the key to the door, but he kept the keys to the elevator and to the fire stairs. Only allowing her out if he needed her for some function or other and even then, he never let her out of his sight. He blamed her withdraw from society on the sudden onset of a rare skin condition that changed, depending who he spoke to. Some believed sunlight caused it, others believed odorous boils she felt shameful of.

When the sacrifice came due, he dragged her kicking and screaming to force her against the door as she refused to spend any time in the living room. Spend any time close to where she felt the hum prickle against her skin, the pull at the little hairs on her arm. He no longer asked for her consent either and just took what he required to appease the room behind the door. Which more and more meant flaying her from scalp to toe. Each sacrifice taking deeper and deeper layers, down to muscle. Weeks passed before she fully healed.

Standing next to the side table, she pulled a packet of crushed angel's trumpet seeds from the little drawer. During the six months of confinement, she cultivated her moon garden in the solarium. Hand selecting flowers for scent and bloom. The angel's trumpet a recent addition, and one with a surprisingly practical use.

She tipped the powder into the empty wine glass as the door to the solarium opened. Gloves, clippers, and empty packet back into the drawer. Wine poured and swished. Taylor coming into view.

"There you are, my love," she said, handing him the tainted wine. "So, what's this about a holdover?"

"The youngest daughter, she's trying to convince her dad not to sell. Says she's heard rumors about doctored financials." Taylor paced, and as he did so, gulped instead of sipped his wine. "A bullshit rumor."

His words came out like a snarl. Then, to Prue's delight, he drained the glass and held it out for a refill. "Our accountants are above board. They know what will happen if they're not."

"I'm sure they are."

"Anyway, because of that jackhole, I'm going to need another peeling by morning."

Prue considered her options of keeping to form and protesting, or going willingly to the door. The articles she'd read online stated the toxin might take effect in five minutes or thirty, depending on dose and personal physiology. Then the dizziness, hallucinations, possible violent outbursts—she hoped Taylor might skip that one—shortness of breath, and, if she got it right, paralysis would set in. Finally, death. In a fortunate bit of luck, Taylor settled the debate for her.

"Whoa," he said, holding out his arms for balance. "Dizzy for a minute there. Guess I should have eaten." He cocked his head. "Did you hear that?"

"Hear what?"

"The door. It sounds like it's singing, but it's never done that before."

She rose and looped an arm around his. "I can't hear it but let's go see."

By the time they reached it, Taylor's gait acquired a lean. Prue released him and stepped back as he crumpled.

He put his hands over his ears. "It's singing so loud."

She crouched down to remove the key from around his neck, but he slapped her hands. "Back off, bitch." He struggled to right his legs but failed. "Why can't I stand? What's happening? What did you do?"

"Ensured you'd never be able to take from me again."

Once Taylor finished ranting at her and fell silent, she attempted to remove the key again. This time his slaps fell short. In her hand, the etchings on the key ignited. The door symbols flared in response. Its power slithered over her. The promise of control, of freedom, of having everything she ever desired.

Prue slid the key into the lock and opened the door. Oh, how wrong she'd been in thinking she knew exactly what lay behind the door. In thinking it only contained black walls and a repeating inscription. This time the room showed its occupant to her, and cloaked as she was in Prue's skin, she was beautiful.

WRATH

I never thought I'd see the day, but we have a Terrace III entry. Wrath typically can't hold their temper past the eligibility paperwork phase, but this year I'm pleased to announce our third-floor rep has broken his eternal streak of pre-competition disqualifications for unsportsmanlike conduct.

Sort Your Plastics You Shitbirds

Performed by Roy the Angry Turtle

I got a lot of problems with you people and you're gonna hear all about it since some of you seem to be confusing our HOME with a fucking LANDFILL but if you take a stroll to the morning lava ponds you'll see a sign the size of your Auntie June's fat ass that says PLASTICS RECYCLING and some simple picto-goddamn-graphic instructions on how to sort that shit but maybe you were dropped on your head a lot as a kid so I'll explain one more Jesus Christing time.

1. *Pop bottles. Everyone knows how much Mountain Dew you fuckin' nerds drink up there on Sloth.*
2. *Milk and Laundry Detergent jugs. Guess we should be grateful the perverts on Terrace VII even wash their sheets.*
3. *Vinyl, tubing, pipe, auto product bottles. I'd also blame this on Lust but I know it's Pride, and while I do have questions, all I ask is that you recycle correctly.*
4. *Laundry baskets, plastic wrap, and bread bags, you gluten intolerant assholes of all levels.*
5. *Yogurt containers, pill bottles, and Jan, I swear to fucking god, if I find one more plastic Starbucks cup left on the benches by the poet pits I'm tossing your furry ass in.*
6. *If the Gluttons want to suffocate in their own chin fat that's their business, just place your Arby's takeout containers in the right fucking bin.*
7. *Look Envy, I know it's you. Toys, sunglasses, all that other plastic gadget shit that keeps you entertained and forgetting that your mothers never loved you. It goes in here.*

And on a final note, kindly breakdown your Factory Prime cardboard before shoving in the paper bin, you fucking barbarians.

Judges' Notes

- Passionate, excellent pacing.
- Such clarity of vision!
- Not a poem.

Score: N/A Entrant is disqualified

THE ENVOY'S BLESSING

CHRIS PATRICK CAROLAN

Vancouver Island, British Columbia, 1880.

Y ou knew the dead man." It wasn't a question.

Nathaniel Garaven looked up from his plate to find the barman looming over him. "Excuse me?"

"The fellow they pulled out of the bay the week before last. Olsen, wasn't it? Word is he was a friend of yours."

"Word travels fast here, Mr. Sutter," Garaven observed. Such was the way in small towns. He had been less than two days in Port Urabus, arriving late the night before last. The boat from Victoria had taken him as far as Ucluelet, followed by several days on horseback through rough country the rest of the way. He hadn't yet had a chance to make many inquiries.

Howard Sutter nodded.

"Well, I'll not deny it when it's so," Garaven shrugged. "Morris Olsen was a friend of mine, yes, and a good friend at that. We fought together in the War Between the States. Hadn't seen each other in a good number of years, but we kept in touch, and it was a letter he sent about a month ago that brought me up this way. I didn't know he was dead until yesterday."

He sipped his coffee and looked around the small taproom. The place was all but empty, save for himself and the barman. Sutter's Rest echoed countless other such places Garaven had seen in his travels — a simple tavern on the ground level with a half-dozen rooms to rent upstairs. At least one of those was occupied, Garaven knew; the sound of violent retching from the next room had interrupted his slumber in the middle of the night.

"Seems wherever I go these days, I find another dead friend."

"You sound like a man with revenge on his mind," Sutter said. If the barman had an opinion about that it didn't show on his face. He had a stern, wind-worn look; Garaven had seen the same stolid expression on working men and women up and down both coasts. Not the kind of man to abide nonsense.

Garaven shook his head in answer. "I've got no stomach for vengeance, Mr. Sutter. I've tasted violence too damned many times, and it always comes back up sour." He drained the last of his coffee. "All I'm after is the truth."

"The truth, is it?" Sutter leaned on the polished mahogany, conspiratorially close. "Do you believe a man can change?"

"Well, friend, depends on what you mean. A man's opinions ought to grow as he learns new things about the world around him. The war taught me that much, at least. But can a man change what and who he is at the core of his being? The things that make him himself? I'd say that's a tougher thing."

Garaven's measured response drew an unexpected rumble of laughter from the barman. "All true," he said, refilling Garaven's cup. "And not what I meant," he added as he slid the cup back across the bar.

"What, then?"

"Lycanthropy, for a start. The full moon's curse, that sort of thing."

"Werewolves, you mean? I saw many strange and horrible things during the war, Mr. Sutter," Garaven said. "Sights that would drive most men to the edge of madness, if not beyond, and I've seen countless horrors in the years since... things a rational mind can't begin to explain." He paused to sip, scratched at his chin. "Physical transformation of the body the way you mean, though? Can a man turn wolf, or burst into a flurry of bats in flight? I've never seen the like, no... but I don't dismiss the possibility, either."

"Stuff and nonsense," came a snort from over Garaven's shoulder. He hadn't heard anyone enter the room, but the new voice came from the direction of the stairs. One of the inn's other guests, then, and a prospector by the rough and wearied look of him. A single purplish bruise the size of a dime marked his cheek.

"You're off to a late start this morning, Mr. Cane," Sutter said impassively as the fellow bellied up to the bar.

"It was a late night," Cane answered enigmatically. He placed a nugget of gold on the bar. "Believe this squares my account for the next month," he said.

Garaven could scarcely help but gawp at the sight of the gold. The nugget was slightly larger than a walnut, and the buttery yellow gleam it gave off in the mid-morning sun told of exceptional purity.

Sutter sighed and paused before pocketing the gold. "Suppose it does, at that."

Cane smirked as Sutter poured him an ale. He upended the glass, draining it in a single pull. The bruise under his eye seemed to grow darker. A trick of the light, Garaven thought.

"*Ahh*," he said, wiping the cuff of his sleeve across his lips. He pushed the glass back across the bar and gestured to Sutter to refill it, turned to grin at Garaven while he waited. "It's all bollocks, you know."

"What is?"

"The shite Sutter is on about. Werewolves and goblins and pixies and whatnot. Storybook nonsense, the lot of it, and anyone who tells you any different is smoking the wrong leaves."

"Or the right ones," Garaven quipped, drawing a hearty laugh from Cane. His own experiences with things uncanny and inexplicable left him short on skepticism, however.

Sutter placed another glass in front of Cane, which he emptied with the same ease as the first.

"Are you not having any breakfast, Mr. Cane?" Garaven asked.

"Call me Lee," Cane replied, tapping the brim of his cap. "I can't stomach food before noon, and a glass of hearty ale's as good as a loaf of bread." He held up the glass and examined it in the light as though weighing whether or not to down a third pint. He set it down and slapped his hands on his thighs before rising to his feet. "Too much to do to sit around here, anyways. The Envoy's blessing be upon you, gents." He made his way out to the street, whistling tunelessly as he left the door to swing shut at his back.

Sutter's eyes had followed Cane every step of the way, Garaven noted, and the big barman's tensed shoulders and tight jaw relaxed with the prospector's departure. Whatever rancor lingered between the two men was their business, and Garaven had no intention of making it any concern of his.

"If you want to know what happened to your friend," Sutter said, "you'd do well to visit the chapel at the end of Trent Street. No doctor in town, y'see, and no real mortuary either, so that's where they took him when he washed up."

"I don't recall seeing a steeple on the way into town," Garaven said. "You mean the big square building I passed on the road? Looked more like a Mason's lodge than a church."

The barman shook his head, looked around as if to make sure no one was within earshot. "A foul place. They call it the Temple of the All and the One," he said. "I'd advise against even walking past it if you can avoid it."

"Is that right?"

"Up to you." He shrugged his big shoulders, turned around to busy himself with some glassware behind the bar. "Chapel's on the other end of town, between here and Wiseman's Rock."

Garaven, figuring he'd get nothing more out of Sutter for now, set to finishing his breakfast.

Something with a hard shell and too many legs scuttled out his path as Garaven made his way north to the chapel on Trent Street. Damp air held the scent of salt underpinned with the same unwholesome odor of dead fish and decaying aquatic foliage permeating every seaside town he had passed through up and down both coasts. He paused a moment, his eye drawn to the desolate scene of the bay at low tide. The receding waters had left moored fishing boats mired, thick black mud clinging to their hulls like tar. Most of the skiffs were in poor repair, as though they hadn't trawled the depths beyond the bay in years.

The chapel struck Graven as small, even for a town of fewer than five hundred. The cedar clapboard exterior had never been painted and the saltwater blowing in off the bay had weathered it beyond its years. The floors and pews and altar within were all immaculate, though, if a bit rustic.

'Immaculate if a bit rustic' also described Father Bilodeau. Youthful and as well-built as any fisherman or lumberjack on the coast, the Jesuit wore both hair and beard trimmed short. He ushered Garaven to take a seat in a pew near the chapel's small altar.

"Yes, I remember the fellow they brought in," Father Bilodeau said, nodding sadly. He spoke with a Québécois accent. "All I could do for him was say a prayer for his soul's repose, unfortunately."

"Could you tell anything about how he drowned in the bay?"

"Drowned?" Bilodeau raised an eyebrow. "*Mais non*, Mr. Garaven. Your friend, he did not drown. He was stabbed several times."

"Are you certain?"

"His body was bloated by the sea and the fishes had taken more than a few bites, but there is no mistaking a knife wound, much less a dozen such lacerations."

Garaven frowned. It was far from the first time one of his friends had fallen to a violent end, but according to Olsen's letter he had only arrived in Port Urabus two weeks before he had written to summon Garaven north. The letter had told of a discovery, but as was typical of Olsen, had been maddeningly scant on details. Had whatever he had uncovered gotten him killed?

Father Bilodeau cleared his throat. "How much do you know about Port Urabus?" he asked.

"Very little," Garaven admitted. "I never knew there was such a place before Olsen wrote to me, and I only arrived here a few days ago."

The Jesuit nodded. "It is an odd name for a town. Urabus. Wouldn't you agree?"

"I hadn't thought about it. I suppose I would've assumed it was an Indian word. No stranger than a hundred other places I've been."

Father Bilodeau shook his head. "It is not an Indian word, but an evil spoken about in whispers. An empty promise made before the time of myth, before the first people made their homes on these shores," he said. "They say it is out there still, slumbering beneath the depths beyond the bay, waiting to return to the world."

"And you believe this?"

"Perhaps it is a tale told to children so they do not misbehave. But I have seen strange things since I came here, and the people, they do not pray to God as they should."

Does a man of the cloth ever think the people he ministers to are reverent enough? Garaven wondered but did not say aloud. "And what do they say this Urabus is waiting for, down there at the bottom of the sea?" he asked instead.

Father Bilodeau's gaze turned to the altar, then to the chapel's rough-carved crucifix which hung above. "I know that answer not," he said, his voice distant. His fingers wound between the beads around his neck as he turned back toward Garaven. "But I fear there are those in the town who labor to see his will done."

The look in his eyes chilled Garaven to the bone.

At Garaven's request, Father Bilodeau had provided the names of the three men who had brought Olsen's body to the chapel. The priest had offered little advice on who to seek first, so Garaven settled on the owner of a local dry goods store, a man named Albert Harrison.

He entered to find Harrison engaged with a customer. Garaven feigned interest in a display of straight razors and assorted grooming products while he waited, but found his eye drawn, more than once, to the woman Harrison was helping. Her beauty was undeniable. Tall and lithe with dark eyes and a complexion as fair as fresh snow, she wore her lustrous black hair pinned high. Along with stylish attire, her striking aquiline features and stoic bearing seemed at odds with the rough environ of Port Urabus.

Whatever business she had with Harrison was conducted in hushed tones. An order to be delivered, Garaven assumed, as she readied herself to leave with no merchandise in hand. She placed a gold nugget on the counter, more or less the same size as the one Lee Cane had used to pay Sutter for a month's food and lodging.

She turned to leave, her eyes narrowing as she seemed to notice Garaven for the first time. "Do you know, Nagualism is but one manifestation of mankind's connection to our animalistic nature," she said.

"I'll bear it in mind," Garaven replied.

The smile she returned was enigmatic. "May the Envoy's blessing be with you," she said, then she was gone.

"What was that all about?" Garaven asked, turning to Albert Harrison.

"You knew the dead man," the shopkeeper said.

"So I've been told," Garaven confirmed. Harrison had dodged his question, but the doings of strange women—even those of great beauty— were not his primary concern. "Seems to be a lot of gold changing hands in this town," he observed.

"Something in the water."

"How's that?"

Harrison shrugged. "Streams around here are lousy with the stuff."

Garaven nodded. From California to the Klondike, some said you could hardly swing a pick anywhere on the west coast without striking a lode. Significant discoveries along the Fraser River and in the Cariboo region had brought countless men to British Columbia's rugged frontier. Some of them found gold, too, though it was a rare fellow indeed who returned to the east richer than when he set out. Far more never returned at all.

"Still doesn't seem like much of a town in the throes of a gold rush."

"Ain't no rush. Folk here prefer to keep it quiet," Harrison said. "Me, I'd be more than happy to have a stream of fortune hunters pass through. You'll make more money selling gear and provisions to prospectors than most of 'em will ever pull out of the ground. But those who have the gold around here... well, they make sure the news doesn't get out."

"Is that what put a dozen knife wounds in Morris Olsen's back?"

"I wouldn't know anything about that. I was one of the men who found Mr. Olsen's body on the shore, true enough. But I couldn't begin to tell you how he came to be there." Harrison shuddered. "Horrible sight he was, too, all sliced up and bloated."

Garaven understood the fellow's unease. He had seen dreadful injuries during the war. The destructive power Richard Gatling's mechanized gun wreaked on the human body was nothing short of horrific, the gross indignity inflicted upon scores of men in mere moments an affront to both God and nature. He had spent the years since searching for the root of the inhumanity he had come to believe nested at the heart of human nature.

"Did you speak with Mr. Olsen before he died?"

Harrison shook his head. "Never met him myself," he said. "A lot of men pass through Port Urabus on their way to someplace else, and they'll stop in for supplies. Your friend, though, he never did come in here. I couldn't tell you much at all about how he spent his time here, brief as it was."

Dinner at Sutter's Rest later that evening was a solitary affair. Sundown had come surprisingly quickly, perhaps hurried along by yet more heavy cloud, and Garaven's day had turned up more questions than answers. As he ruminated over stewed beef and potatoes and a glass of ale, he wondered how he would uncover the truth around Morris Olsen's murder. If anyone in Port Urabus knew anything about it, they were keeping it to themselves.

He took a long pull of ale. Small towns always held secrets, he mused, and why should Port Urabus be any different? Albert Harrison had said the locals closely guarded any knowledge of gold to be found in the region. It was certainly a secret worth killing to keep. Could it have been the discovery Morris Olsen had written about?

If so, it made little sense. Olsen had never cared for wealth. Following the war, he was one of the dozen men who along with Garaven had set out in search of answers about what drove men to commit acts of evil against one another. Fifteen years had yielded five dead friends and very few answers.

Movement outside the window caught his eye. Half a dozen figures cloaked in black shuffled past in silence, hoods drawn up to conceal their faces. The head of the line swung a golden censer as he walked, thin trails of silvery smoke issuing forth.

"What is that?" Garaven asked.

"The Wednesday procession," Sutter said from behind the bar. "Devotees of the All and the One."

Garaven watched the small group slowly make their way up the street. "The All and the

One. That's the temple you advised me to avoid this morning?"

Sutter nodded, once, the expression on his face unreadable. He turned and left the room before Garaven could ask anything further.

Garaven woke to the sound of thunder from below. Sitting upright, he rubbed at his eyes as his fuzzy wits grappled with that. *Thunder from below?*

It was another few moments before he remembered he was in a bed in a rented room on the second floor of Sutter's Rest. He swung his legs over the edge, jammed his feet into his boots. Not thunder, then, but whatever calamitous noise had roused him had come from the taproom downstairs.

He heard further thrashing as he headed for the stairs, the sound of wooden furniture being knocked over. He hurried down to the dining room.

The fire on the hearth had burned down to embers but the lamps were still lit. Whatever violence had raised such a ruckus had ended by the time he got there, but the aftermath was plain to see. Tables and chairs had been upended and broken, leaving splinters of wood laying scattered across the floor. Shattered glassware and crockery added to the debris.

Sutter lay on the floor, his back popped up against the bar. His clothes were a shambles and he bled from a cut above his left eye, a purple bruise welling up below it.

"What happened?" Garaven asked as he knelt at Sutter's side. "A robbery?" He glanced at the door, saw it was bolted. None of the windows had been broken. If anyone had entered to assault Sutter, they hadn't forced their way in.

"I held out so long, Mr. Garaven," Sutter said, sweat and blood running down his face. His skin had lost much of its ruddy hue.

"I don't understand," Garaven said. "Held out? Against whom? What do you mean?"

"You've wondered why everyone in Port Urabus pays for everything with gold."

Garaven nodded.

"It's the Envoy's blessing," Sutter said. "It's the gift we—"

Another coughing fit more violent than the last overtook Sutter before he could say any more. His body convulsed against the bar. Garaven held his handkerchief to the taverner's mouth, but Sutter pushed him away with surprising strength for a man so afflicted. "Stay back," he said between pained wheezes. "I was a fool to let damned jealousy and greed overstep my better sense. But when everyone you know has so much more than you, and you've worked twice as hard for what little you have... well, what is a man to do? Stay back! You don't want to let it get to you, too."

"I still don't know what you're talking about," Garaven said.

Sutter's belly heaved and he pitched forward. His jaw hung slack for a moment, then his bile rushed forth and out to splash on the floor. Instead of stomach juices and bits of his last meal, his sputum was a murky whitish liquid flecked with half a dozen shining yellow pellets, none of them larger than a pea.

Gold, Garaven realized.

Sutter struggled back to a sitting position, his back against the bar, gasping for breath. What little color his face still held had faded to a ghostly, waxen pallor and the purplish mark on his cheek darkened and bulged and began to swell as if being pushed out from within. The skin below his eye split open as a spherical black mass the size of a dime forced its way through.

Garaven recoiled as the rest of the thing emerged, a writhing scarabaeiform. Its skin–if it was skin–was a dull white streaked with flecks of black. It wormed its way through and out, half the length of a man's forearm in all, leaving a coagulated dry socket on Sutter's face in its wake.

Garaven scrambled to his feet and took several steps backward as the larval thing inched its way down Sutter's heaving chest to the floorboards. Whatever senses it possessed, it seemed to know Garaven was nearby. Its wormlike body tensed and extended as it advanced toward him, a thin trail of clear slime in its wake.

His back against the wall, Garaven kept his eyes on the thing as he sidestepped his way along. His hand came to rest on the cold, rough stone framing the taproom's hearth and he glanced down, spotting the set of fireplace tools. Turning his eyes back to the creeping thing, he grasped blindly for whichever came first to hand, coming away with the hooked poker.

So armed, he thrust the length of iron between himself and the creature. It gave no sign it noticed the implement or perceived it to be a threat.

Garaven reeled his arm back and brought the iron poker down on the creature, connecting with a rubbery wet *thwack*. It gave no cry of pain but recoiled spasmodically. Garaven struck it again, then again a third time. He rained frenzied blows upon the thing, splintering the floorboards in the effort.

Finally, the twitching ceased.

Sutter lay slumped on the floor, babbling and delirious. His breath came in shallow, rapid gasps. Once more he heaved, ejecting another half-pint of the milky sputum pebbled with tiny pellets of gold.

"Half the town, Mr. Garaven," he said, his voice barely a whisper. "Half the goddamned people in this town carry the Envoys."

Garaven clutched his shirt by the lapels. "Is that what that thing was?" he demanded, pointing to the gray-black smear he had left on the floor.

He might as well have saved his breath. Sutter gasped once more before slipping into unconsciousness.

"Looks to me like the Envoy withheld its blessing."

Garaven turned at the sound of the voice, spotted Lee Cane at the bottom of the stairs. The prospector leaned against the wall, a pistol dangling from his right hand. He pulled out a pocket watch.

"Follow me, Mr. Garaven," he said. "If we hurry, we can be there before the ceremony begins."

The clouds overhead cleared as Garaven followed Lee Cane through wind-stripped cedars and out toward the rocky shore in the shadow of Wiseman's Rock. Stars brighter than stars hung in the sky, the largest among them aligned with the full moon. Cane had hurried Garaven along at a good clip and had not been particularly conversational during the hike from Sutter's Rest. "It's just a little further," he said now.

"Where are you taking me?"

"You'll see soon enough." The pistol hadn't left Cane's hand. He hadn't aimed it at Garaven in that time, but the casual way he held the weapon with his finger on the trigger implied all the threat Garaven needed.

Torchlight edged into sight as they crept around a bend, and Garaven saw the ceremony Cane hinted at. Seven figures stood around a tidepool perhaps fifteen feet across. Six were clad in black cloaks — the procession from the Temple of the All and the One. The cloaks had concealed their faces when they had passed Sutter's Rest. Now their hoods had been pulled back. Each figure's face was concealed by a mask of gold, almost featureless aside from simple slits for the eyes.

At the center of the semicircle stood a female figure clad in a brilliant red cloak hanging open at the neck. Even at this distance Garaven could tell she wore nothing beneath it. Only after closing the gap by several more paces did he realize she was the woman from Albert Harrison's dry goods store.

"The Sleeper awakes," the Priestess declared, raising her hands to the sky.

"The hour grows late," the chorus of black-clad figures replied.

"The moon and the stars align," she said, and her followers dropped to their knees. She turned and seemed to notice Garaven for the first time. "Does this one seek the Envoy's blessing?"

"I seek only the truth," Garaven replied. "What is all this? What happened to Morris Olsen?"

"The truth, is it?" she asked, torchlight illuminating a bemused grin. "The All and the One reward those who willingly serve, but the Sleeper rejects an impure Host."

"The Host was impure," the chorus replied.

The Priestess regarded Garaven, the expression in her eyes at once speculative and seductive. "Will you accept the Envoy's blessing?" As one, the six black-clad figures extended hands to usher him forward.

Garaven felt the barrel of Cane's pistol in the small of his back, urging him to the edge of the tidepool. Below the water's glassy surface, the tidepool teemed with life. Anemones and urchins and things he couldn't name clove to rocks dotted with tiny starfish and waving plants. Gazing into the thriving microcosm, he felt awed at the diversity of life existing here in careful, isolated balance.

Further down, a fissure split the rocks. A swirling gray-white mass nestled within the crack caught his eye, a hundred writhing, intertwining fingers silently ululating in the depths. Garaven's stomach churned at the sight, but he could not avert his eyes.

"Your choice is of little import," the Priestess said, "for soon, Urabus rises!"

The tidepool's surface rippled as though a stone had been thrown into the center.

"He rises! He rises!" the chorus exulted.

Garaven watched as something black and octopidian unfurled from the fissure at the deepest part of the pool. It broke the surface of the water, a slithering tentacle several yards in length. Its skin was a glossy obsidian black, smooth and featureless, seeming to drink in the moonlight as it extended.

The very tip of the thing approached the Priestess. With whatever sense it possessed, it reached out and touched her chin as a lover might caress his paramour. She shivered at the thing's touch.

"Let this one be the sacrifice!" the black-clad figure nearest to Garaven shouted, reaching out to clutch at his arm.

Garaven swung his fist in a wide arc, solidly connecting with the side of the man's head. The golden mask came loose and fell to the ground, revealing a face unlike any Garaven had ever seen, a twisted visage from some dark nightmare.

The man—if man he was—had skin the iridescent whitish pallor of a salmon's belly and six eyes. Two of those were normal human eyes in the usual place, but above and below these were narrow slits, bulging and blinking with glossy black irises. He had no real nose to speak of, just nostrils, and an unnaturally long chin split vertically by a lipless orifice which opened and closed as he grunted in pain. The lips of another mouth—this one in its proper location—were wrapped around what looked to be a gold nugget the size of a fist.

Garaven felt his stomach sour at the sight of the monstrosity's face, but pressed his advantage. His foot shot out, catching the fiend in the gut. His foe doubled over and heaved, milky sputum gushing out the corners of its mouth where the gold nugget remained firmly stuck. Whatever evil had twisted his form so, he still felt pain when struck in the usual places. Garaven grabbed for the man's cloak, spun him around, and dropped to his knee as he pulled on the fabric with his full strength. The wrestling throw—a holdover from his schoolboy days—pitched the twisted figure into the tidepool's waters.

"No, you fool!" the Priestess cried out.

But it was too late. The full length of the unearthly tentacle writhed as if lit afire when the man entered the water. He struggled to get his feet under him, but the tentacle lashed toward him and wrapped around his neck. He cried out just once before being dragged under the water, disappearing into the fissure.

A hue and cry from the chorus was cut short as more tentacles broke the surface, darting like black lightning toward the gathered figures. Garaven watched in horror as the cloaked men were ensnared, lifted skyward, then pulled into the tidepool to join their compatriot. In less than a minute, only the Priestess remained.

Garaven looked over his shoulder. Lee Cane had retreated several paces, his face ashen. He held his pistol high but aimed at nothing. Well, what could he aim at? Garaven was simply glad Cane had the presence of mind not to fire off rounds blindly.

The Priestess dropped to her knees at the tidepool's edge, weeping. "The moment has passed, and I have failed, failed," she said between sobs, her face held in her hands.

The black tentacles once more broke the surface of the water, slithering toward her. She looked up, then, and in the moonlight Garaven saw the black marks on both of her cheeks. Dozens of similar spots appeared all over her body, her naked skin mottled with black and purple splotches blistering like swollen urticaria.

Her expression turned from one of grief to exultation, even ecstasy as the tentacles from the tidepool wound their length around her body. She shuddered as they worked their way up her skin, wrapping around her neck and head until she disappeared under their weight. The writhing mass of muscle and sinew paused a moment, holding her in its embrace before retreating into the water. The Priestess was gone.

Garaven felt a hand on his shoulder, turned to see Lee Cane at his side. The scoundrel had tucked his pistol into his belt.

"What in the name of Hell was that?" Garaven asked.

"Urabus, I suppose," Cane shrugged, "or at least part of him. I don't rightly know, if I'm being honest, and I don't think we would've wanted to see any much more. Way I understand it, there was a very specific ritual to be performed at a very specific time on this very specific night to bring him fully into the world. Showing up when we did spilled the spittoon into the soup pot." He knelt to pick up a rock, which he tossed into the tidepool. Nothing happened.

"It may be just as well," he said with a wink. "I like the world well enough as it is." He turned away, wracked by a sudden coughing fit. Pulling his hand away from his face, he spread his fingers to display a small lump of gold, slick with saliva and mucous. He handed it to Garaven.

"For your troubles, Mr. Garaven," he said. The bruise under his eye darkened and bulged. "Plenty more where that came from."

Lee Cane turned and strolled off down the beach, whistling tunelessly as he disappeared into the darkness.

SLOTH

Well, well, well, look who finally crawled out of their den a day late and a dollar short. Did you finally get a job besides acting fourth floor rep, while Fern and Clover are off on a dam building mission to create yet another stagnant pool no one asked for? No? Don't give me that I-can't-adult-today garbage. Toothy rodent. Just spill your dreadful guts and slink back to your mud hole.

Can't Play, Won't Play
Performed by Scout-Fig Fennel the Millennial Beaver

This mesh network sucks
No bandwidth, high latency
Cry myself to sleep

Judges' Notes
- I hate mesh networks.
- Could be busier.

- I feel your pain, but not your soul.

Score: 3/10

EAT THE RICH

SARAH L. PRATT

Josie knuckled her nose against the decay wafting from under the pool cover. It retracted slowly, exposing brown water to the sunshine already scorching her shoulders. Glancing around the coiffed gardens surrounding the Tuscan revival, an open septic tank seemed out of place to say the least.

When the spring-cleaning query came through the Summer Sisters website, she'd noted the tony Tarzana address and quoted high, expecting to get hammered down as usual. The client's only response was in the form of a bank transfer. Paid in full. And now she knew why.

"Smells like a gas station toilet," said Vern, her Raggedy Ann braids swaying as she cranked the cover into a fat roll of slimy blue vinyl. Then she stood back, tugging her yellow bikini out of the crack of her perfect peach. "Did they say it would be this scuzzy?"

Josie grabbed a skimmer, dipping it through the curdled surface. "We can't turn down paid work, not after Waller Prince stiffed us. Jesus…I'm not even sure what this is."

"With a pool this gross their money is probably worse. They're probably mean."

"Anyone with money is mean, Vern."

"We should just go. I'm starving."

"And how are we gonna pay for your insane In n' Out habit?" Josie asked. "You need to cut back on those milkshakes anyway. You're gaining weight."

Vern shrugged and adjusted her triangle top. "Just goes to my tits."

Josie fumed as she skimmed. Plain with brains in her modest two piece, she couldn't look at a burger without getting bloated. Little sister on the other hand, beautiful and bless-her-heart-dumb, ate like a bear during salmon season, and only ever seemed to get more voluptuous, more supple, just…more. She thrust the skimmer aside. "We're gonna have to drain."

Josie's crocs crushed through the well-hydrated turf as she made her way to the side yard and entered the code on the key pad fixed to the pumphouse door. The interior was gloomy but sterile and expensive machinery hummed as it attempted to rinse hopelessly fouled water.

"Oof…" An eggy odour from the floor drain burned her sinuses. The client mentioned they'd been away for "some time". Long enough for something to move in and die in their pool.

She made her way to the control panel, trying to breathe through her mouth. First, she shut down the filtration and conditioning units so as not to set off alarms. Draining a pool in Los Angeles was not something you did lightly. Not that Summer Sisters' clientele gave a damn about the planet. They'd shit a bowling ball at the bill though. For all the money these idiots wasted on ten-step skincare they sure as hell were a bunch of tightwads when it came to home maintenance.

The premium she and Vern charged wasn't for their ability to unclog a filter. Anyone could do that. But two hot chicks in bikinis jousting with skimmers on the pool deck? That was luxury. That, they would pay for. For a while. Josie examined her breasts snuggled in black spandex. Less perky at 38 than they were at 30. Even Vern's goddess looks had a shelf life. Every spring-cleaning season came with an acute reminder that time was running out.

She needed to work smarter, not harder. Waller Prince, that insta-rich crypto bro, racked up a huge invoice, summoning them every week to mop up after his disgusting parties. He personally supervised their work from his poolside chaise, airpods jammed in his ears like an insect, ogling Vern behind his shitty Oakleys. Their van needed a new transmission and tires. Rent had gone up. They needed money and he knew it. So, she shouldn't have been surprised when he not only refused to pay, but threatened to sue them for damaging his property—which Josie had when she'd chucked a paving brick through his windshield, but who could blame her? Fucking asshole. Who knew fixing a Tesla could cost so much? Now they were in trouble. Now they owed serious money to the last person she should have borrowed from.

With the push of a button, a woosh and gurgle filled the sewer pipes, eliciting a gust of rotten air from the floor grate. Whatever had infested the works would be flushed soon enough. Satisfied, she wandered out to the mansion proper. Large windows bare of coverings. People with money wanted you to see inside, and she expected this client's interior to be straight out of central casting like Waller's. Neutral palette, modern art, and uncomfortable sofas. Kitchen with a glacial slab of marble, bowl piled high with lemons that wouldn't dare sprout a fruit fly.

But this…was not that.

It was dark. Darker than it should be with the windows wide open. Dark wood floors, tables and cabinets. Every surface littered with what at first looked like curio shop bric-a-brac but on closer inspection was the real deal. A trio of shrunken heads, shelves of books so old they'd vaporize if you blew the dust off them. Sculptures and paintings of animals mixed into grotesque combinations. Pottery covered in strange markings.

"What?" Josie whispered. "Who are these people?"

Across the living room, through the windows on the other side, Josie saw Vern skimming out muck into a bucket. The retro Walkman clipped to her bikini bottom dragged the band down on one hip revealing a strip of pearly skin below her tan. She grooved along the pool deck, red braids flaming in the sun.

They could have expanded their business, hired more girls to clean pools. Newer, younger, hotter. But Josie would feel more like a pimp than a boss. Besides, most of their business was word of mouth. And those mouths all wanted Vern.

With the client suitably distracted. Josie would often sneak into the home to divest the place of any bit of treasure unlikely to be missed. Never jewelry, never an expensive watch, but silverware was often to be found in unsecured abundance, as was crystal, and just about every house had a drawer of old phones and tablets, full of precious metals, and discarded after the release of a new model or a collision with the travertine.

Josie tugged and the door slid open with a soundless glide. The way no patio door in her cheap apartment experience ever had. When you were rich, everything was smooth and weightless. She wanted that. For herself and Vern. They'd earned it.

Another quick check to ensure Vern was still doing the blissed-out boogy with the skimmer. But she wasn't. She was gone. Josie slid the door shut and raced around to the pool deck.

"Vern?" She scanned the shrubs and topiaries. "Come on, where you at?"

No answer. Only the humming grind of the pumphouse as it sucked filthy water out of the pool.

"Vern!" Josie dashed along the perimeter of the yard. This wasn't right. It wasn't right and an electric lash of panic cracked through her bones. "Veronika!"

A splash and Josie whirled to see her sister erupt from the pool like a sewer-dwelling Venus.

"The fuck—"

Take care of Vern. Take care of your sister. She needs you.

And she always had. Even before mom ran off with her drug dealer, even after children's services discovered they were on their own and Josie scraped together some money and they lit out in the night, headed for LA. She never let anything happen to Vern. Never let her go hungry, a feat in itself. Josie always found their way out of a jam, and only rarely resorted to handjobs to do it. They'd since built their business up to something as successful as possible given the deck was stacked against them in just about every way.

"Something was jamming the inlet." Vern clambered out of the water, holding a melon size clump of hair in her fist.

"Why the hell would you jump in there?"

"Didn't you hear that grinding?" Vern started picking apart the sodden hairball. "The pump was gonna burn out. I tried to get it with the skimmer but it wouldn't budge."

"That smell is never coming off you." Josie coughed at the dirty stink as she peered at the mass of hair and saw a yellow glimmer. "What is that?"

Vern clawed at the dense mat. "Jewelry?"

Traditionally, clog components were finder's keepers. Rich folks liked to swim in their bling and they'd scammed more than a few diamonds and pearls from various filters.

"Just about got it," Vern growled, her brow crumpling in a way that made her look cutely determined rather than old and disapproving. "There!" She wrenched her hand free, holding a slender, 6-inch spire of serrated gold.

The skin on the back of Josie's neck puckered in a sudden chill. "Oh my god."

"Whaddya suppose this is worth?" Vern held up her hand and a look of confusion clouded her eyes as she noted the stream of crimson sluicing down her arm and dripping onto the pristine Brazilian Ipe. "Oh…"

Josie clutched Vern's elbow, swiping the blood from her palm long enough to reveal a deep slice running down her lifeline into the vascular lacework of her wrist.

"We need to get you to a hospital."

"Isn't that expensive?" Vern asked.

Josie felt the sting of failure once again. Decades working her ass off, and still no health insurance. One of the many reasons they couldn't afford employees, the premiums were larcenous.

"Ow," Vern whimpered as Josie probed, fresh blood flowing as quickly as she could swipe it away. Deep, but not arterial, at least she didn't think so. Still, a large puddle had pooled on the deck, never mind the bacteria taking root with every passing second.

"Inside. Now." Josie smeared the patio door with gore as she yanked it open. They dripped scarlet as they went, checking all the kitchen cupboards, and finding them entirely empty. "There must be a bathroom, a first aid kit somewhere."

They turned down a dim hallway, trying door after door, all locked. All but one. It was just a closet. An empty closet. What kind of weird-ass people lived here?

Vern reached out, steadying herself on the doorframe. Josie heard the distinctive click of an electromagnetic lock release and the back of the empty closet swung open.

"Whoa," Vern said.

The room was lit by a black candle and over the smell of rancid pool water and blood, floated something woody and vegetal. Incense. On a table with a purple velvet runner was gold object. A head. Half human, half jaguar, maybe a bear, its face twisted in rage or pain. Maw hinged open, a long, serrated fang on the right, and on the left a broken stump.

Vern held the gold blade in her non-wounded hand and frowned as she regarded the snarling idol. "It looks hurt."

Josie's existence spun on its axis. She'd learned to recognize these moments. The ones where you could walk away, continue on the path you'd been treading, or you could take a left and change your life. No legit collector hid their acquisitions in a closet with a false wall. This was Sketch City and Josie wasn't interested in the tour. Her skin crawled as the damp fragrant air coated her pores.

"Jo-Jo, I don't feel good," Vern mumbled as she collapsed, braids wrapping around her like the cut strings of a marionette.

"Vern," Josie grabbed the idol, warm to the touch and somehow soft, as though the gold were a malleable clay and the creature didn't always wear this sneer of agony. She set it aside and yanked the velvet runner off the table, wrapping Vern's freely bleeding hand with it. Vern's skin was clammy with the pale shimmer of steamed white fish. "Fuck this, I'm taking you to emerg."

Vern moaned. "We don't have the money."

They really didn't. Goddamn Waller Prince. "Don't worry about it, Verny. I'll figure something out."

"N'just hold it right there."

Josie turned to find the beam of a flashlight slicing into her retinas. "It's not what it looks like," she said and for once it really wasn't.

"I just bet," said the voice, a man trying to sound official but not quite selling it.

Josie could handle this. "Sir, if you get that light out of my eyes, I can explain."

"Don't try anything," the man said. "I got a taser on you and I'm authorized to use it."

Damn it, they must have tripped a security alarm.

"Come on out, slowly," the man said as Josie hoisted Vern to her feet and they awkwardly squeezed past his anonymous bulk into the hallway.

"If I'd known our client had security I would have asked to be let in," Josie said, shuffling ahead of the man into the living room.

"I wasn't born yesterday, girls. Why don't you have a seat while I call the authorities."

Josie led a delirious Vern to the couch and sat her down, refolding the partially drenched runner over her arm. "Look, officer—" She turned to see a white boomer in ill-fitting chinos, a Costco polo and a lanyard that said only "Jeff" with some kind of polic-ey shield logo underneath. In his hand he held a black stun gun.

"You don't look like a security guard," Vern slurred.

"I lived here long before the swells moved in and I keep an eye on things."

"You made your own laminated badge," Josie said.

"Mouth off then, see where it gets you." He fumbled for his phone while keeping the stun gun trained on them like it was a Glock.

Having located a weak spot, Josie pressed harder. "Before you make that call, how are you going to explain why YOU entered the premises?"

"Beg pardon? You're the intruders."

"And are you the homeowner?"

"I'm the Citizens Watch."

"You're a nosy neighbor." She nodded to the stun gun. "And you threatened us with a deadly weapon."

Jeff flushed a diaphoretic rose. "I saw two girls trespassing onto private property for a little stealth pool party. I'm going to let the police sort this out." He thumbed his phone open.

"Jeff," Josie said. "Let me explain, and if you still feel the need, you can call the cops."

Jeff's tired eyes narrowed. Now Josie was the one sweating. If the cops showed up there was a chance they could string together a dozen petty theft reports and link them to Summer Sisters. Goddamn Waller Prince. She would have walked out on this job the second she saw the condition of that pool. If she hadn't borrowed 5K from the meanest drug dealer she knew.

Vern slumped against her.

"Jeff," she said again—men liked hearing their names coming out of a woman's mouth—as she leaned forward, breasts threatening to tip out of her bikini top. She cursed herself for not going with something stringier. Vern smelled like a cattle farm tailing pond. She was usually the secret weapon but today it was all on the significantly less hot sister. "We were hired to clean the pool. Our van is parked behind the house."

"Last time I checked the pool was outside the home, miss." Jeff folded his golf-tanned arms over his chest, wrist sporting a very nice Omega.

"I know we shouldn't be in here." Josie extended Vern's arm. "But there was a sharp object clogging the filter and my sister is badly cut. We were hoping to find a first aid kit is all."

Jeff's jaw slackened. "Well why in hell didn't you say so?" He sat beside Vern, taking her arm so gently in his large dad-hands that it made Josie's eyes sting. "Let's have a look, honey. I got full first aid training."

Jeff bent his balding head over Vern, tenderly unwrapping the purple runner and examining the slash across her palm and chuckling. "Now that's a classic bagel cutter right there."

A rumble emerged from Vern's stomach and she blinked, suddenly alert, sitting up straight. "Can we get milkshakes now?"

"Soon as we get you fixed up, okay?" She mentally calculated how fast they could extricate themselves. Jeff was neutralized for the moment but she didn't want to push their luck.

Jeff shook his head. "Not even that deep. Have a look."

Josie's laugh caught in her throat when she leaned in, examining Vern's palm where indeed the cut was healing by the second.

"Well, I'll be damned—" Jeff's voice cut off in a squeak and a spray of blood fanned across Josie's face. She lurched back to see Vern's jaws opened impossibly wide, clamped around the back of Jeff's neck, ripping out a baseball size chunk of meat and a few vertebrae. Jeff gurgled and dropped lifeless into Vern's lap.

"Vern!" Josie screamed but Vern only growled and violently swallowed what she'd taken. Again she dipped her head, jaws pried open and snapping like a bear trap on the rest of Jeff's head, taking it apart piece by piece.

Blood raced into Josie's temples, drumming away in a mad stampede of platelets. How was it possible for Vern to swallow something so much larger than her own throat? And her face, distorted, jaws unhinged in an agonized silent scream of hunger. Just like the idol.

Jeff's head was gone. Josie crawled into the far corner of the couch, closing her eyes and covering her ears, but couldn't block the sound of ripping flesh, the stony crunch of bones, and the great guttural gulping as Vern devoured the rest of the unfortunate neighbour.

Tears washed through the blood crusted on Josie's cheeks. She knew this job was bad. Knew it. No one paid that quickly and in full. And some of them didn't pay at all. Fucking Waller Prince. Fucking rich people. They were all freaks. Greedy freaks. Now they'd taken the only thing worth anything to her.

She wasn't going down for this. And neither was Vern.

Josie grabbed the purple runner and slipped down the hall to the secret room where she wrapped the golden idol in the bloody fabric. When she returned to the living room, Vern sat cross-legged on the sofa with a smile on her face. No sign of Jeff, no clothes, no bones, and weirdest of all, no blood. Not a single drop.

"Now can we get milkshakes?"

Pulling up to their North Hollywood apartment, the crappiest building in the best neighborhood they could afford, Josie put the van in park and sighed. "What just happened?"

"I dunno," Vern shrunk into her seat like a puppy about to be swatted with a rolled-up newspaper.

"You ate a guy," Josie said, staring out the windshield at a Saab being broken into by two kids barely old enough to reach the pedals. "A whole guy, in like eight bites."

Instead of explaining Vern convulsed and turned her head out the window spewing a dark torrent of vomit. Her body heaved once again before stilling. She pulled herself back inside the van wearing a bib of black ooze and holding a platinum Omega in her teeth.

Josie placed her hand under Vern's mouth and she dropped the watch.

"Jeff would have been proud of this," Josie mused, turning the slimy timepiece over in her hands. The inscription read *Bon Voyage*. "Guess it's true that nothing'll kill you faster than retirement."

Vern sniffled and wiped the effluent from her nose. "I never wanted to eat a person before."

"Yeah. That's definitely new."

"I was so hungry, and he tasted so…rich." Vern's pink tongue peeked out, swiping the corner of her plump lower lip.

Josie clutched her sister's dirty hand, fingers twined in calloused familiarity. "It's going to be okay. We've got that thing," she jutted her chin at the bloody wrapped bundle in the back, "and we're gonna figure this out."

The kids deserted the Saab, leaving the doors hanging open. Josie would have normally made a half-hearted gesture at chasing them off but today was anything but normal.

They trudged up to the fourth floor where the smell of salami and cabbage never seemed to dissipate. In their practiced choreography, Josie slid the key into the lock and Vern tugged the door tight to the jam to ensure it actually opened. Once inside, Josie placed the bundle on the kitchen table, marched Vern straight into the bathroom, and filled the avocado green tub.

"God, you smell like a zoo." Josie cannonballed a bath bomb into the water and any offensive odors were swiftly smothered by a thick pillow of tutti-frutti, Vern's favorite.

Once immersed, Vern studiously scrubbed at the pool crud, vomit, and residual Jeff, while Josie began the crusty work of unravelling Vern's braids. Once loose they splayed out like threads of blood in the fruity water. Each time she blinked, Josie saw the image of Vern's wide open jaws crushing Jeff's skull. There was no washing that away.

And what to do with that golden monster head? How soon would the police get involved? Skipping town cost money and fugitive life was a cash only business. They were going to need every penny they could get.

"Someone's at the door," Vern whispered.

"Huh?" Josie's fingers stilled in the suds crowning Vern's head. "You sure? I didn't hear anything—"

Bang, Bang, Bang. A fist heavy enough to punch the door right through the cheap frame. Josie cringed. She knew that knock, and it wasn't the cops.

"Josephine!" came the muffled bellow. "I know you're in there, you sneaky bitch. Open up!"

"Fuck," Josie said, wiping her hands on a towel.

Vern reached out of the tub and grabbed her leg. "Don't answer it, Jo-Jo. Stay here."

"Don't worry." Josie said too brightly. "Migrainz is all bark. I can take care of this."

Josie padded over the disintegrating carpet to the door, opening in a crack, keeping the chain on. Glowering down at her, below a pompadour Elvis himself would die for was a 6'7" mountain of a woman, half as wide as she was tall, and topping Josie's list of people not to be fucked with. "Um, hey. You know it's not such a great time so—"

The door flew open, knocking Josie on her back. Dazed, she stared up at the water-stained ceiling.

"You said Tuesday." Migrainz hauled Josie up and pinned her against the wall. "It is now

Tuesday, the sequel. Where's my money?" Her surprisingly fresh breath puffed in Josie's face.

"Funny story," Josie squeaked.

"Well I ain't running a comedy club. So we may as well cut," she flicked open a switchblade, "to the happy ending."

Josie's vision bleached around the knifepoint aimed at her pupil and her heart redlined into a rhythm too fast to follow.

"I like happy endings."

Migrainz and Josie turned their heads to see Vern, all clean and wrapped in a tiny white towel.

"Well hey, sis," Migrainz said with a grin.

"Vern, don't—"

Migrainz choked Josie off with a massive paw, heavy rings digging into her larynx. "Sweet of you to come to your deadbeat sister's defense, hon. But unless you got five large hidden under that towel, someone's gonna be using her bikini as an eyepatch."

"Follow me," Vern said, amber eyes glowing in the dim light. "Maybe we can find a way to be friends again."

Migrainz' grip loosened and Josie gasped, "What the hell are you doing?"

Vern gave Josie a smile. One Josie had never seen before. Gone was the usual guileless innocence, the sunny foolishness, and in its place was... Josie always suspected Vern was asexual.

She was so childlike it was hard to imagine anything different. But something had changed, and now her sister was hungry. Hungry beyond the appetite for burgers and shakes.

"Maybe I've been doing business with the wrong sister," Migrainz said, flinging Josie back to the floor. "Always had a soft spot for you girls."

Josie lay on the sour carpet, struggling to fill her lungs with air as Vern and Migrainz disappeared down the hall. It wasn't long before a low moan sifted through the walls, concluded by a single yelp.

When Josie got up the courage to creep down the hall to Vern's room, she found her naked on her bed sucking the last drops of Migrainz' blood from her bath towel.

Vern looked up with glassy eyes. "My body is going through changes."

"This isn't like getting your period."

"I just didn't want Migrainz to poke your eye out."

"I know, I know." Josie shook her head. "Get dressed and pack anything you can't live without."

Vern started to nod, then shuddered once, twice, her rosy skin blanching. Josie was about to admonish her not to puke on the carpet, but that didn't seem to matter much at the moment. Not like they'd be coming back to claim their damage deposit.

Vern pushed past her into the bathroom. Josie followed in time to witness Vern disgorge into the tub an unholy tide of brownish black muck that seemed to groan as it leapt from her body in chunky gouts.

Vern collapsed on the floor and Josie gathered her into her arms, yanking another towel off the bar and wiping her sister's face clean. Vern shivered, and gagged once more. Josie expected another flag of black vomit but Vern reached into her mouth, farther than it seemed she should be able to, and pinched from her throat a greyish wad of pulp, banded with a silver M.

"Is that…" Josie scrutinized the damp bundle. "Migrainz money clip?

Monogrammed titanium wrapped at least ten thousand in hundreds, a little damp but otherwise in good condition. Migrainz carried her stash on her person. Not trusting any hiding place above her ability to pulverize potential muggers.

Josie peered into the spattered tub, recoiling at the familiar stench. "Guess we know what happened to that pool."

Josie tried not to tap her foot impatiently as Fiver gave the idol a long inspection, touching it only as necessary, lifting it only to assess weight and density. As always, he struck Josie as being much older than his mere twenty years. A slight young man in his uniform of navy coveralls and white trucker hat, rattling about in the small metallurgy shop where he could make, or unmake, anything from engines to earrings.

He swiped the pristine brim of his hat. "Where'd you say you got this?"

"I didn't" Josie said, pulling the front of her tank from her sweaty chest, feeling sticky and unclean in Fiver's fastidious workspace. "Do you know what it is?"

Fiver tipped the idol back revealing an odd sigil inscribed on the bottom. "This is a maker's mark. I've only ever seen pictures but my Abuela said it means 'The Factory'."

"What, like a cheap trinket made in Taiwan?"

He shook his head, a dark look clouding his face. "The watch I can fence, but folks trafficking in looted artifacts, especially Factory artifacts, don't exactly advertise in public Facebook groups."

"Actually, I was hoping we could use your kiln."

Fiver's naturally wide eyes frogged out even more from his boyish face. "You wanna melt it?"

Josie threw up her arms. "You do this all the time."

"To ugly class rings, and clumps of gold chains shoved in the back of some rich white lady's jewelry box. Your basic snatch n' grab kit. Not this. We could get beheaded in some countries. Desgracia." He concluded, crossing himself for good measure.

"It's just a hunk of gold." Josie tried hard to keep her voice from shaking. Trying to sell Fiver on the notion that this was business as usual. "Since when are you superstitious?"

"Since my Abuela told me don't go messing with any god you can't call by name and especially not one that comes from la Fábrica."

"I'll give you forty percent by weight." Josie followed Fiver's gaze to Vern, who'd hopped up on an oil barrel, chipping at the paint with her fingernails. Fiver, like the most of men, had a hopeless crush on Vern. The only difference was that he might be the only person Vern might possibly crush back, in her own first-day-of-kindergarten way. "We're in a real jam here, Five."

"Jo-Jo says we gotta disappear," Vern chirped. "Like a rabbit into a hat."

"Think the rabbit gets pulled out of the hat, Verny." Fiver sighed and shook his head at Josie.

"Okay, you're the boss. But I'll just take my usual twenty."

"Are you sure?"

He didn't dignify that with a response as he pulled a pair of tongs out of an aluminum trash can full of iron bars bent to various purposes. From anyone but Fiver this refusal to gouge would have been an affectation. A performance of virtue. A way into Vern's bikini bottoms. But it was Fiver, and Fiver was clean as his stupid hat. He'd never cut you a deal, but he'd never cheat you either. He was basically a kid, but the closest thing the Summer Sisters had to a friend.

He lifted the idol, carried it across the shop and slid it into the kiln. "This is gonna take a few hours."

Josie nodded and sidled up to Vern. "You good?"

Vern nodded. "Can I have a juice box?"

Fiver puttered about his shop, calling out answers when Vern asked him for help on the New York Times crossword. Vern had surprisingly extensive memory banks but couldn't spell for shit. Josie used Fiver's laptop to google possible hideouts in Mexico, where their gold would stretch the furthest. She looked up to see Fiver opening the kiln and reaching in with his tongs.

"We got a problem," he said.

"Huh?" Josie rushed over, wincing at the volcanic heat boiling out of the kiln. The idol sat defiant, and completely unmelted. "How is that possible?"

"It isn't," Fiver said. "Gold melts at just under two thousand degrees. That thing ought to be a puddle of slag."

"Maybe it isn't gold." Vern said, standing behind them, stroking her lower lip with the gold fang she must have held onto in all the chaos. A line of drool dribbled down her chin. "Maybe it's something much, much worse."

Josie drew in a sharp breath. Fiver wasn't a threat, he was their friend, Vern loved him. And she'd just eaten.

"Fiver, get back" Josie said in a low voice. "Run."

But Fiver didn't get back. Fiver didn't run.

"You on something?" he asked Vern.

"I'm hungry," she pleaded in a halting voice, tears streaming from her eyes. "Fiver, please…"

"Hell, you don't gotta cry. There's half a pizza in the fridge. Yours if you want it."

Was he blind? How was every primitive flight instinct not activated by the sight of this predator. The low growl in her throat, the sickening click of her jaw, and the sharp shine in her eyes as she assessed her prey.

In the end, Fiver went quietly. Maybe enough of Vern remained to insist on mercy. The last thing he ever saw was the thing he'd wanted the most. Vern, rushing into his open arms. A swiftly broken neck ended his fantasy and then he was no different than the others. Unzipped like a garment bag and emptied out one organ at a time. Liver, lungs, reams of intestines, and his sweet young heart. Reduced to so much meat, gristle, and bone, tossed down Vern's distorted gullet as fast as she could swallow.

Josie waited in silence, forcing herself to watch Vern devour every morsel down to his white hat. Fiver deserved that much. He deserved a witness.

Vern cried as she threw up into an empty trash bin. "I'm sorry," she wailed between heaves. "I'm sorry, Fiver."

Numb, Josie used the tongs to fish a small silver crucifix from the pool of black slime. For all the glitter and gold he handled for his clients, this was the extent of his extravagance. Just like Jeff and Migrainz, the only thing left of Fiver was the most precious thing he owned.

Josie wrapped the crucifix in a rag and stuffed it in her pocket, silently promising to get it to his madré. Then she pulled the idol from the kiln, setting it on the iron anvil. It was body temperature to the touch. She glared at its lopsided sneer, lip curled up over the ragged stump of its missing fang.

"What are we gonna do?" Vern asked, still sobbing over Fiver's liquified remains.

Josie reassessed their situation. Without Fiver they wouldn't get much for Jeff's watch. And Migrainz' 10K wouldn't last long, even in Mexico. She had to take care of Vern. And no fucking way was she going back to the desperate hustle of the old days. Sweaty creeps in their stifling cars, the gamey smell of leather and sex.

"We're putting this thing back where we found it," Josie said. "But first we're going to pay a visit to Waller Prince."

Vern's head popped up. "Why?"

"We need an out. And there's no fatter pig just waiting to be served up on a platter."

"I never ate anyone on purpose," Vern stated, not conflicted, just factual.

"Think of it as a last meal. If this works the way I think it does, I'm betting you chuck up his crypto wallet password. This is our ticket, Vern. We can disappear and never pick up a skimmer again."

The van cruised slowly past warehouses and trash strewn gutters, up into the hills with lush boulevards, McMansions, and high desert air smelling of clay. Finally they reached the palace gate, behind which the Little Prince lived. Josie took it as a sign when her code still worked. As she crept up the drive that led to the servant's entrance, her stomach seemed to fill with concrete.

This was the right play. An animal has to feed, right? Why not someone who deserved to be eaten?

Josie parked the van and squeezed her eyes shut. Jeff and Migrainz were self-defense. Fiver was an idiotic accident. Waller Prince though? Sneaking up to his house with the intent to teach the spoiled dickhead a lesson he wouldn't live to forget? That was pre-meditated murder.

"We can't do this," Josie groaned, slumping over the steering wheel.

"Why?" Vern unbuckled her seatbelt and scooted closer, bringing with her the scent of blood.

"This isn't us." Josie sat up, touching Vern's cheek. "It's not you. I can't let you go down this road."

"But you said disappearing costs a lot."

"Maybe we don't need to? No one can connect us to Fiver, Migrainz had plenty of enemies. A missing suburban Jeff is trickier but...well, no body no crime right?" Josie raced down the line of logic with distinctly un-Josie optimism. "We can take this thing back, and forget it ever happened. Write it off as a bad gig with a cash bonus."

Vern shook her head, red braids flailing. "It's too late for that."

"I can take care of this. I promise. We'll get our money out of Waller some other way."

"But I'm hungry."

"Verny, no."

Vern sandwiched Josie's hand between hers. The sweet touch of the sister she was before she developed the ability to chew through a human femur.

"You always take care of me, Jo-jo. Now it's my turn."

Josie looked down to see her skin parting as Vern dragged the gold fang across her palm, biting into the rich red meat of her.

AVARICE

Next up, tower denizens, we have an extra special treat. Coming off a century ban for the excessive misuse of the word *cevere* in a non-consensual and unsportsmanlike manner, our beloved fifth floor rep has graced our ungrateful presences with a delight torn directly from the bottomless void that is her passionate, ejaculating heart.

An Exultation for Supremacy
Performed by Jan the River Otter

I triumph
*and ascend the golden halls of my **ancestors**,*
*observing the morose **epitaphs** chiseled upon the*
*granite slabs gracing the **bulwarks** of decay*

*how art thou come to this **residence***
*of **wonder** and achievement*
*oh **daughter** severed*
*from the river of **dream***

*by the **timeless** yet infinite*

*I bask in the **glory** of his approving ministrations*
*fur **glistening***
*eyes **gleaming***
*claws **glittering***
***head** held high*
*the aura of perfection blasting **radiance***

I am
*beyond **all***

Judges' Notes

- Bravo Madame!
- My heart swoons in both grief and joy for the light that no longer shines in this dim, dying world.
- No point continuing, this can simply not be surpassed.

Score: 11/10

ATTACHMENT

SHANE KROETSCH

Fernen steps around me as he scans the message scratched into the concrete wall. Fixing his attention on the closing, he pauses.

I hope you are well.

I hope you are unafraid.

Good-fucking-luck with that.

He wipes his nose with the back of one gloved hand and tucks his notepad under an arm. The cover is worn and curled at the edges, the pages stained with Christ knows what. He carries it everywhere and produces it at a moment's notice like he's an alternate dimension marsupial. Instead of offspring, the pouch in his armpit holds half-formed ideas of a perfect world. Fucking poets. Always trying to either prove or disprove how existential everything is. You'd think they'd all be in hell where they belong, but here we are, me and Fernen — an utter failure and Purgatory's Poet Laureate.

When Fernen walks past, his eyes twitch back and forth, never focusing on me. He's got something on his mind, and that never ends well. I hang back and, not for the first time today, consider how I got here. It sounds ridiculous, but I made a New Year's resolution to love and be loved. Given a less than fifty percent chance, how could I not have been doomed to fail? I fell off the wagon, then fell from grace. Years of hard work went down the drain along with the contents of my stomach. What wasn't purged got stuck in my throat, like I wish my words had that night, then maybe I wouldn't have ended up here.

Fernen slinks away, past the crude graffiti depiction of an angry river otter humping a human skull and around a corner. I unzip my jacket and the layer under it, dig a soft leather square out of the inner pocket and bend it open. In times past, it would have held dollar bills, credit cards, or maybe a condom. Now it's empty, save for a dogeared picture. I tug on one corner, pulling it up just enough to see the eyes. Someone I used to know. Someone whose memory takes the space of so many other things, like how long

I've been here. Sure hasn't been a thousand years, but it sometimes feels that way. Especially without her by my side.

I hear Fernen circling back, so I tuck the picture, stash the wallet, and zip up. He leans around the broken wall, focusing on my hands resting at my sides.

"You coming?"

"Yeah. Two seconds."

He forces a dodgy grin. "You just can't help yourself, can you?"

I shrug and reach into my pockets.

"Don't be like that. We're almost there. You'll have your chance to find her soon enough."

"I know."

He nods and disappears again. I tuck my thumbs under the straps of my empty pack and hop forward to catch up.

Past the crumbling brick wall of a derelict warehouse, Fernen crouches beside a weed-riddled mound of dirt. He waves me forward and down, urging me to keep out of sight. We're closer to the Tower than I've ever been. The glare of the polished gold exterior is abrasive. More so when you take in what exists around it. Poverty and filth. Pain and fear.

Fernen reaches for his notebook, opens the cover, and starts scratching away with the nub of a tooth-marked HB pencil. When he's done, he pinches his thumb in the hinge to keep the pages flat and clears his throat. "The weeping willow sways. As tears fall, like leaves from its branches."

He calls it four-count-eight. Says he created it. Says if he had gotten around to publishing a book of his work, it would have revolutionized short-form poetry. He would have been famous. That's great and all, but it's hard to give feedback on something you don't understand, and I ran out of positive things to say about it a long time ago.

"How is that even poetry?"

Fernen scowls. "What?"

"I mean, it doesn't even rhyme."

His jaw clenches. "It doesn't have to *rhyme*." He waves his free hand. "We've been over this a hundred times. I'd explain it to you again, but at this point, I know you won't get it."

"Is it because you're as bad at explaining as you are at writing poetry?"

His face flushes. The soles of his boots pivot in the dirt as he turns away, spitting an inaudible insult.

The hint of a smile I allow to break through my raging anxiety doesn't stay long.

Fernen leans close to the mound and stretches his neck out to see around it.

I peer over his shoulder to confirm what's captured his attention. A thin woman in a simple black dress, holding a plain black purse to her chest, steps out from the columns and statues flanking the tower's entrance. Thick sunglass frames eclipse her gaunt face, and stringy grey hair lays flat on her head. A stick figure of gloom framed by elaborate opulence.

Fernen tucks the pencil and the notebook back into their home. "That's her."

It's hard to tell from this distance, but the tightness in my chest confirms it's true.

A tank of a sedan with tinted windows careens to the curb in front of the entrance. The driver lumbers out, hat askew and jacket wrinkled, shows the woman to her seat, then rushes back to their spot behind the wheel. They spur the machine around, through the heavy gates out front, and disappear into the distance.

Fernen faces me, the pain of my comments regarding his creative endeavours already forgotten. "Told you. Same time, every day."

My sarcastic congratulations stick behind the lump in my throat. A rare break in the overcast sky allows a narrow beam of dismal light to reach the tower's fifth floor. If all goes well, my ticket out of here resides behind those walls. I understand the contradiction of stealing to get into Heaven, but I need to see her again. I need one more chance.

Fernen is watching me. I swallow hard and answer his next question before it's posed. "Let's get this over with."

The solid steel exterior door snaps open, and Fernen catches it before it slams closed again. His eyes focus behind us, watching for signs that the first step of our break and enter might have been noticed. Slowly, he faces the gloom inside, raises a haphazard hand to usher me forward.

Dim emergency lights offer enough of our surroundings that I don't fall down the concrete steps leading us below grade. We swing wide around thick steel pipes rising from the floor and wander past the humming walls of the generator room. Fernen hangs a sharp left down a corridor lined with colour-coded roll-up doors. Behind them, sorting machines process mountains of discarded packaging left over from endless Factory deliveries and the remnants of the broken things they replace. He quickens his pace while grazing the wall to his left. I skip to catch up but lose sight of him as he bends past a corner. I barrel on ahead but trip over myself when I make it around.

"Jesus fuck."

Fernen spins to face me, hands out from his sides.

I back away from a spider the size of a dinner plate scurrying up the wall.

Fernen frowns. "Seriously?"

My chest heaves, fighting to absorb enough oxygen to satiate my pounding heart. "Did you see that?"

"They get big down here." Fernen's eyes trace the shadows around the ceiling. "It's the humidity or something." He turns and, without another word, continues on.

Another metal door caps a short passageway. Fernen glances through the woven security wire filling the small rectangle window set to one side. He turns to me as he pushes his back against the silver bar, and the latch clicks open. Shooting me a sly grin, he rushes on.

By the time I walk through, Fernen is already at the end of the next poorly lit passage and up a short set of steps. His body hunches forward. I can't see his hands. I hear a click, and a panel on the wall beside dims from green to red. The heavy door in front of him opens. When I reach him, he has a foot stuck through to stop it from closing.

"What the hell was that?"

"What are you talking about?"

"Don't give me that bullshit. How did you get it open?"

Fernen's shoulders drop, and he tilts his head back. He holds one hand out from his side. A white plastic keycard is pinched between the knuckles of his pointer and middle finger. "I got tricks, man. I told you."

I fight the twitch building in one eye. "Where did that come from?"

"I have a talent for finding the things I need." He looks away. "As long as I'm okay with paying the price."

Before I can ask, he continues, "Anyway, it's done. The card is a clone. Even if the system tracks it, nobody will know something is off until we're long gone."

"I don't like it."

"You worry too much."

"Who else knows we're here?"

"Nobody." He eyes the card before stashing it in his pocket. "I've had this forever. I was just waiting for the right time." He reaches out and taps my chest with the back of his hand. "And the right partner."

"If we were really partners, I wouldn't be finding out about things like that while we're in the middle of it."

"Don't worry." Fernen shrugs. "It's a small detail. The situation is under control."

I'm tempted to ask why he even needs a partner when he seems to have it all figured out, but the opportunity slips past, like a freight train without a driver.

"I help you. You help me. Isn't that the way it's supposed to go?" Fernen steps through the door into warm light. He holds it open and glances back at me. "Are you coming or not?"

"Yeah." Tightening the grip on the straps of my pack, I snatch the door handle before the latch grabs. Crisp air tinged with a hint of black licorice washes over me. The kind my grandmother used to leave out in a crystal bowl on the coffee table. I hated my grandmother. I rub my earlobe, the one she used to drag me around if I acted in a way she disapproved of. Stepping onto the intricate pattern of the carpet, I watch the door shut behind me from the corner of my eye.

Fernen is halfway down the hall, standing under a glowing halo. Once he knows I've seen him, he pushes through another door. He doesn't wave at me, just keeps moving.

Along the corridor, overhead lights bloom and fade as I pass. The stairwell access sign shows we're almost there. Except, it doesn't feel like it at all.

Past the door, Fernen pauses with one foot on the floor and one on the second step up. He's bent over, scratching in his notebook. When he's done, he rests one elbow on his knee.

"Each step brings near, a hint of the destiny I long for."

I sneak a glance behind me. "We should get going before somebody sees us."

Fernen stashes the notebook. "Sure."

We power on, up and up. The only conversation is the alternating clicks of our soles on the painted concrete treads.

Fernen leans beside the wide slab door with 548 engraved in gold font, the keycard held out and waiting. "You ready?"

I'm not sure if I am, but I get the feeling it's too late. "Yeah. Do it."

He waves the card above the doorknob. The latch clicks. He presses down on the handle, swings the door wide, then moves over to offer me the right of way.

I try not to hesitate as I step through, moving to one side. Fernen backs in beside me and closes the door.

It's nothing like what I expected. Instead of the best and finest, it has the feel of someone's first home, pieced together from thrift store bargain bins. Meagre fixtures scatter around the foyer, the only distractions from the copious amounts of dated wood panelling. Beside the entrance, a brass coat rack holds a bent wicker sun hat. I look past it to the cherrywood entrance table, its finish worn through on the legs. A ceramic vase is on top with a bundle of dead flowers, sitting crooked within. Not just dead but hung to dry—an impression of beauty frozen in time. Above the flowers, a group of faded photos in tarnished frames fan out over the wall. While Fernen wanders off, scanning the ceiling, I lean in for a better look.

A happy couple on their wedding day, each with a crumbled piece of cake in their hand, ready to strike.

The husband with longer hair and stubble on his chin. A proud father, holding his daughter for the first time.

A close-up of the baby girl swaddled in a thin blanket. One blue eye, and one hazel, shine like a clear summer morning.

The girl's first birthday party. She's in a frilly dress. Her ribbon belt matches the bow on the present beside her. Her smile is one people would say will break hearts one day.

As the trail of pictures continues, the girl's round face and chubby arms give way to adolescence. She's riding on her father's shoulders, a pink balloon hovering above, keeping watch over them.

Adolescence gives way to maturity, and the smile is still there. The father leans over from the passenger seat of the family car. The young woman's white knuckles are perfectly positioned at ten and two.

She's in a blue gown, raising a rolled-up piece of paper in one hand, the other holding her father's tight.

Now she's laughing, pointing a camera at the one taking a picture of her. The reflection in the lens is stretched and distorted but clear enough.

Images of the mother are rare. She exists in the background, not looking at the camera. If she's on her own, it's to model a new piece of jewelry or favourite outfit, the most common being a fur stole over a fitted black dress.

The last of the pictures are small and tucked at the bottom. The father is thin, eyes deep. His skin is as near transparent as I've seen, somewhere between a living man and a ghost.

A tap on my arm shakes me back to the present. Fernen points a thumb down the darkened hall, stretching away from the entrance. "I'm heading in."

I nod. Fernen fades into the shadows. I take one last glance at the beginning and end of a life, then follow.

The hall looks more like an art gallery than a scattering of family pictures. Gilded frames, perfectly spaced, have small lights perched above. Rich mahogany floorboards spread out under my feet. Wallpaper with the texture of fine linen shrouds the walls. The story of a life continues with each step forward.

The woman, with one blue eye and one hazel, rests a hand on the hood of her first new car. Sun glints off metallic paint and polished chrome. Next, she leans against the doorway of her first house, a modern bungalow with a perfectly manicured lawn.

It takes me a second too long to figure out what's different. She's lost her smile. That fact is harder to notice as the pictures continue. Better car. Bigger house. As subject matter, the woman gets smaller and smaller until she's gone altogether.

The remaining pictures only show places and things: white sand beaches and crystal water, designer fashion, a sprawling estate complete with stables and tennis courts. Something feels wrong about them. It's like those pictures you see at Halloween—from one angle, a beautiful portrait, but from another, a zombie with rotting flesh dripping from its bones. Here, the images are pristine and fresh, but underneath, I sense cracks in the façade. I get the feeling if I tilt my head, I'd be able to see the half-finished work and neglect.

Over my shoulder, the hall winds out of sight. I don't know how long I've been walking or how far ahead Fernen is. I picture a labyrinth spiralling deeper and deeper to its heart. The reason why that image doesn't bother me never fully forms. The apartment didn't look that big from the outside, but sometimes these things are hard to gauge. Rubbing at the fog settling in behind my eyes, I press on.

Further down the hall, I pass under an archway, similar to one you'd find in a garden or a cemetery. The walls darken and buckle in on themselves. No longer elaborate, the deep, wooden frames hang crooked on the wall. The first few are empty. Images manifest as I press forward, but they are unclear or abstract. The last before a wide gap in the wall shows a screaming face as if pure torment has been given shape.

I lean through the opening into a cramped room. Two velvet chairs face each other in front of a marble fireplace mantle, and the biggest TV I've ever seen hangs over it. It looks like it hasn't been used in a while. Nothing does. Thick dust covers every flat surface. Spider webs sprawl from every corner. Shuddering, I sneak a quick glance at the walls on either side of me as I back away.

I continue, the tips of my fingers dragging along skewed walls. The frames here hold no images behind glass covers. Instead, they surround crude wood carvings, a rusty knife, a sailing ship made from shed horns, and piles of tarnished coins, the kind with square holes in the center.

A pair of ten-foot-tall solid oak doors stand square at the end of the hall. Angling in, they offer enough space to walk between without rubbing your elbows. I pass through but stop just inside.

Even the never-ending hallway, and the weird shit that lines it, hasn't prepared me for what waits behind the doors. Bookshelves, as tall as redwoods and as wide as a city block, fan out in every direction. Each has a rolling ladder attached and is overflowing with every shape, size, and colour of book imaginable. It's not just in front of me either. They line the perimeter of the room, if that's a sufficient word to describe it. Narrow entranceways lead to other rooms filled with more shelves and even more books. A twisting staircase leads to a second floor, then another. Floor upon floor soar and blend into the distance, well past the point of counting how many. A pentagonal stained-glass ceiling as big as the sun filters insufficient orange light over everything below. Fresh ink hangs sharp in the air as if hidden pages are still populating with words and thoughts yet to be explored.

Fernen may not have told me everything, but I know what we came for. Books of the rare and expensive variety. I pull the pack from my shoulders and leave it on the floor. Guess I should have brought something bigger.

I wander the rows on the main level until I find Fernen. His head is down. His cheeks are red, and his chin quivers.

"I seek love, unrequited. My heart to fracture, to never want again."

I make sure he's done before I dare speak. "That's a little dark."

"I wrote it." He closes the book. "I mean, I would have."

"What, like you would have if someone else hadn't got to it first?"

He shakes his head. "No. If I had lived longer." He looks up and around us. "This library is the penultimate collection of the written word. Everything that exists but also hypotheticals — books never written, scripts never acted. Where good ideas, forgotten ideas, live on forever."

I search the shelves until I find a name I recognize, a favourite from my youth, and reach for the first in the stack. The cover is pristine. My hands may be the only ones in existence to have cracked it. The copyright page shows it's a first edition, printed in 1926. Scanning the others, I settle on a title I don't recognize. Another first edition, this one printed in 1976. Except Hemmingway died in 1961. I may not know much, but I know that.

"Is this some kind of joke?"

Fernen clutches his book with both hands. "It's really not."

My head fills with pressure. Even though I don't know how to start processing what this place is, I give it my best shot. That's why the faint sound of footsteps behind me doesn't register until just before the old woman speaks.

"It is quite impressive if I do say so myself."

When she takes her glasses off, I'm transfixed by one blue eye and one hazel, though their once vibrant light is a distant memory. Her smile is as crooked as the pictures of her journey to this place. The fact that she's not upset to find us here does little to ease the panic vibrating through my body.

"Beyond the realm of our base needs, each of us accumulates possessions for different reasons. To feel important. To fill the emptiness inside. What we forget is that for each new treasure, for every new moving part we add to our existence, something must be given in exchange. Occasionally, it is our time or attention. Other times, what is taken is a small piece of who we really are." The old woman fans a brittle hand. "That is one of the reasons I am still here. Too much of my soul is fractured. With that in mind, I saw no point in stopping."

She walks away from us and to the wall stretching from the entrance. "It took some time to understand the possibilities once I arrived here. Not only how to rebuild my collection, but how to truly make it one of a kind. That is when the fun began."

I break my gaze away from the old woman and take in the entirety of the entrance wall for the first time. Gnarled spikes run through seemingly random objects, holding them to the pale, mottled surface of the wall like keepsakes stuck on a pincushion of bloated flesh. A gold watch. A ring of car keys. Above each object is a photograph showing a single face. None of them seem to be enjoying themselves.

I zero in on a spike twice as long as the others, stacked tall with gold wedding rings. The picture hanging from the end is filled with a round face, caked with makeup and topped with messy, artificial blonde hair. The woman's wide-set grey eyes focus hard on me. One corner of her thin lips turns up.

A cell phone with an endless social media feed scrolling behind the shattered screen hangs nearby. The man in the picture above has hints of silver at his temples, but his skin is taught, showing he's had more than a bit of work done. It's hard to tell, but I think he's mouthing *help me*.

A familiar fur stole hides near the corner. I can't see the face in the picture nestled inside. Silver hair hangs around the skeletal hands covering her eyes, but I would recognize it if I could — the mother. Her shoulders quiver as she sobs.

I lower my head, angling toward two cameras hanging from another jagged hook and the space above them where a picture should be. The polaroid camera doesn't hold my attention, but the old point-and-shoot does. The last time I saw it, it was in the hands of the father.

"When you say your collection being one of a kind, you mean...."

The old woman is steady, unmoving. "Souls are more tangible than a figure on a bank slip. They don't require the maintenance a stable of horses or a garage filled with vintage automobiles do." She motions to the rows upon rows of books. "They certainly don't require a great investment in space." She offers me a shallow wink. "At least, not yet."

I glance sidelong at Fernen. "What the fuck did you do?"

He won't look up from his feet. "I told you. Everything has a price."

I force myself to breathe. "Yeah? What was the price this time?"

He shakes his head.

"*Fernen.*"

His lips twist down, trying to escape the words about to pass across them. "You. The price is you."

My hands shake. I don't even know what to say. Fucking self-absorbed, cock-sucking poets. Nothing is more important than their own fleeting bullshit.

Fernen cradles his book tight to his chest, and he wails. "*I just wanted to know I was good at one thing.*" He rests his chin on the leather edges, then bites down on his lower lip. "This was the only way. She said I could have it. I—I'm so sorry."

The old woman slips out of her shoes and lets her glasses drop to the floor. She lifts the polaroid camera from its hook and rests the strap over her outstretched neck. "A long time ago, I learned that when it comes to acquiring, the pool is only so big, and the benefits of being creative with the search are many." She angles the camera so it points at Fernen. "Plus, there are only so many visitors that never leave before the neighbours take notice." She presses the red button on top.

I don't see the book hit the floor, but I rub away the echoes of blinding light in time to see the old woman kneel while she waves the developing picture at her side. The floor where Fernen stood is empty.

She straightens with Fernen's book in her hand, slides a fingernail between the pages to open it, then tilts her head and reads. "On scraps of paper. I elevate my soul but manifest my end." Her crooked smile, with yellowed teeth, now gapped and pointed, widens. Her eyes, one blue and one hazel, bulge from her skull. "How appropriate."

She snugs the picture between the pages. I get one last look at Fernen and the tears staining his cheeks as she closes the cover. Good-fucking-riddance.

The old woman faces the wall. Her free hand stretches and contorts. The nail of her pointer finger solidifies into a twisted spike with a jagged hook at the end. Bone-pale legs splay out from the bottom hem of her dress as her body elongates. Her shoulders hunch, flecked with thinning hair. She holds the book up against the wall, stabs through it with her deformed nail, then bends her hand until it snaps free.

The old woman's upper body arches in my direction. Blood drips from her hand and pools on the floor. She doesn't pay it any mind. The only thing she cares about now is me. "Why are you here? I understand the writer and his motivation."

I could run. Nearly every bit of me wants to, except my feet refuse to listen. My mouth is struck just as dumb.

She tilts her narrow face. I feel like she's seeing more of me than I want her to. "Love or regret?"

I clear my throat. "Both, maybe."

Her eyes pierce the shell of my jacket to where I keep the wallet. "Show me."

My last bit of resolve drains away. Whether Fernen told her or not doesn't matter. Nothing does, really. I look down and suck back my sorrow before it spills over. Taking out the wallet, I pull the picture free and hold it in front of me.

"Beautiful." The word slinks from her mouth as though she should be licking her lips. "You loved her?"

"I still do."

"Are you sure?"

My eyes snap to hers. "What do you mean?"

Her pointed shoulders shrug. "If you loved her, you would have been there for her in the end."

I'm speechless, except for two words. "Fuck you."

Her warped smile renews. "Wanting, the need for attachment, comes in many shapes. And, what we hunger for isn't always material." One spider-like claw cradles the bottom of the camera. "Amassing possessions and loving another person are the same instincts with different names. They are expressions of power, of control. Do not delude yourself otherwise."

A dry throat prevents my last formed thought from being shared. As a reflection glints across the camera's lens, I close my eyes tight, not wanting to see what comes next.

"It's okay to be afraid." She lets out a grinding cackle. "It makes for a better picture."

Click.

GLUTTONY

Sorry folks, I know it's been a long ass day already and you've all been impatiently waiting for the final two contestants even though it's obvious we already have a clear and unassailable winner *cough* Jan from Terrace V *cough*. As I've mentioned twice already, I was having trouble prying Terry from the gender-neutral water closet at the far end of the lava ponds where he'd apparently barricaded himself since his ill-fated cookbook Crowdfunder, but I've managed to coax him out with a ton of shrimp and the promise to replace his stupid Parrot. Whatever.

Linda (A Lament)
Performed by Terry the Shark

O universe! O Linda! O submerged cage!
At whose twisted wires I despair and rage,
Quivering at the thought of now and then.
When will I ever see your splendor back onstage?

Never again — Oh, never again!

In the Tower night and day
A table set for a solo buffet.
Wretched prayers, hagfish slime, and a final amen.
A box of bones, a box of decay
Never again — Oh, never again!

Judges' Notes

- FFS Terry, just… stop… crying.
- Surprisingly upbeat. For Terry.
- Uh, Percy Shelley here again, what the hell?
- Piss off, Shelley, we've already determined nobody gives a shit.
- While mildly derivative, I'm starving. KFC anyone?

Score: 7/10

HARES AND HOUNDS

LINDSAY THOMAS

I can't claim to be bored. Boredom would be something, a sentient recognition of time, a shiver, a stirring of breath against skin, anything, something.

But this. This is nothing.

A monotone haze of mediocrity arranged in consecutive order.

Like millions, I have sold my time for the next fifty years to the highest bidder. In exchange I am afforded the great privilege of a roof – rented, food – packaged, and the time-honored tradition of paying taxes.

I'm told that I should be grateful. Plenty of people have less. A thought that conveniently neglects to mention that plenty of people have

more. Is it not normal to want more? To simply —
want?

Lying in bed, the alarm screeches next to my ear. I haven't turned it off because I'm staring at the water stain on the ceiling. I should call the Super, but I probably won't.

The wall behind the headboard rattles with the pounding of fists so I slap my hand over the clock and drag back the sheets. Ignoring my slippers my feet press into the cold floor, goosebumps scatter over my legs.

Shower, toast, coffee, commute. A bus occupied by lifeless fares. Even the teenaged mother stooping over a stroller looks particularly grey this morning.

When I arrive at work Angela has already started the morning tasks.

"The tetras need cleaning. Some died over night," she says as she counts the float into the cash register.

I hang my jacket in the staff room and pluck a net off its hook. Three neon tetras are dancing in the water current, their tank-mates darting around them, indifferent to the corpses.

I hold the net close and examine the fish. Gossamer fins lay limp, their namesake vibrancy fading under pinpricks of white.

Angela is sweeping the floor, as she does every morning, as though I tracked in a desert's worth of dust on my heels.

"Ich," I tell her, extending the net forward.

She drops the broom and snatches it from my hands. "Seriously? Fuck." She strikes the net against the garbage can, the fish tumbling to the bottom. "Quarantine the tank, there's an anti-parasitic under the counter. And sterilize the net, would you?"

I reach for the net.

"And Kevin, don't splash any of that aquarium water anywhere, okay?"

I do as she asks. I always do as she asks. The model employee. Punctual, quiet, nodding when I should, appropriately frustrated when necessary. At least I have a few days off after this; enough time to stare at the water stain some more, maybe even call the Super. It's good to have dreams.

The tanks are scrubbed and water changed, fish fed, shelves stocked. A child comes in asking for a Nemo fish, her father asking if it can live with her guppies.

I'm elbow deep in old tank water when Mikey arrives for the afternoon shift. He's 45 and the exact picture of where I don't want to be: stoned, broke, and perfectly content to live and die in Jolly Rogers' Fish Emporium.

He disappears into the back and re-emerges wearing his employee shirt, mop and bucket in hand.

"Do anything fun last night?" He drops the bucket and gets to work on a puddle where my syphon had slipped, spewing water over the floor.

"Watched paint dry." It's not far from the truth. "You?"

He rings out the mop. "Played Halo and passed out."

I continue scrubbing the sides of the tank.

"Do you game?" He's mopping on the other side of me now. There's a fluorescent light buzzing overhead.

I shake my head. "At least not recently. Not since high school."

"What about real-life games?"

I pull a rag from my belt and wipe my hands. "Like, board games?"

The mop splats onto the tile, spraying water over our shoes.

"More like wide games, like Capture the Flag."

"Sure." I tuck in the rag. "When I was ten. Why?"

Mikey props an elbow on the mop and scratches his stubble. "There's a game happening tonight. I'm supposed to bring someone."

"That doesn't sound like my thing, thanks though."

"There's a prize." He leans in. I can smell coffee and weed on his breath. "It's a lot."

"What's a lot?"

He straightens. "Dunno, just that it's a lot."

"What game is it?"

"All I know is that we're supposed to meet outside that old industrial site outside of town – the one that flooded a few years back."

"How do you know about this game, and not know about it at the same time?"

He leans in again and I back into the tank sending ripples through the water.

"I sometimes surf the dark web."

I raise an eyebrow.

"Not like that, Jesus Kev. I just like to see what's out there, you know, the stuff most people don't see. Aliens n' shit."

"Thanks for the invite but I have plans tonight."

"Your paint can't dry on its own I guess." He continues slurring grey water over the floor.

I pivot to restocking shelves, helping customers between bottles of dry fish food, water filters, blood worms in the freezer. The afternoon is a steady stream of FAQs with the occasional showdown between store policy and the customer is always right.

"No, ma'am, you can't put a fish in a tank the same day it's set it up. Yes, ma'am I understand it's for your fiancé. I'm sorry your engagement party tonight is ruined, ma'am."

It's three o'clock and I'm getting ready to punch out, aware that the fleeting sense of relief lightening my chest is because I'm leaving, not because I'm going home.

On my way out I pass Mikey labeling the new cichlids.

I've regretted most things in my life up until this point; Fractured relationships, fragments of college degrees cobbled together into a compendium of debt, never quite fusing into anything meaningful, a haphazard writing career that went limp before it even began.

So, sure, why the fuck not?

"Do you still need someone for your game tonight?"

Mikey pops the lid back on his marker. "I asked Angela but she has a date. He drops to a whisper. "Between you and me that defeats the reason I asked her in the first place. Two strikes in one blow, man."

"I'll go." I immediately wish I could swallow the words, inhale them into my lungs like smoke.

He claps my shoulder. "Right on. Nine o'clock, outside the industrial complex, and no phones."

"Seriously?" I shove my hand in my pocket, making sure I didn't forget it in the staff room.

"Apparently if footage gets out it spoils the game."

I shake my head but agree, nonetheless.

On my way out I stop to pick up my paycheck, wave to Angela, and drift into the long shadows of late afternoon.

Mikey is already there when I arrive, leaning against a ladder stretching up the side of a looming building, iron and steel dull with neglect.

"Hey," The standard greeting someone of who doesn't know what else to say.

"You made it!" He pushes himself up with the flat of his foot. "I was half wondering if you'd changed your mind."

"I considered it." I still am.

"Everyone else has gone in. You ready?"

I nod and let him lead the way.

Through the main doors stretches a mildewed hallway unfolding into a vast room littered with debris and discarded equipment. In the centre of the room is a stage rigged with dozens of screens, rising to the roof, stacked in rows.

Twenty, maybe thirty other people are milling about, mostly in pairs.

We join the others, waiting, for what I don't know. Mikey doesn't seem to know either.

After several minutes the lights above us blink the room into darkness. The screens stretch and distort, then sharpen. A face crystalizes; Venetian-masked in monochrome-white, their voice garbled like a dying woodchipper.

"Welcome to tonight's event. For those who have not played before, please look at your fellow participants."

"There's people here who have played already?" Mikey whispers. "That's not fair."

I glance at the strangers flanking me, the screens flushing their faces in ghostly blue. The pulsating glow shrinks the room somehow, it feels darker, closer. I notice a man nearby, bearded, electric light gleaming against a bare skull. Had he crawled from between scenes of American History X, I wouldn't be surprised. His long arms are crossed over his chest, smothered in tattoos that I can't make out. He notices that I'm watching him, and I look away.

"Half of you are hares. And half of you are hounds. If you were asked here by someone, you are a hare. If you asked someone here, you are a hound. This space is 75,000 square feet. Cameras have been set up in every room, stairwell, and hallway."

The screens flicker and cut to hundreds of cameras haunting derelict offices and the yawning voids of corridors.

"Hares: It's your objective to make it through the night. Hounds: It's your objective to make sure that they don't."

"Sounds easy enough," I whisper back. "Like hide n' seek."

"You are not to interfere with another hare or another hound. Doing so will result in immediate termination. Trying to leave will result in immediate termination. Any attempt to communicate with anyone outside this building will result in immediate termination. The Hares who make it through the night will be rewarded accordingly. The hounds who successfully terminate their hares will be rewarded accordingly."

The screens flip to a pallet sitting in an empty room, bricks of cash stacked upon bricks of cash.

"Five Million Dollars," the voice says evenly.

My palms begin to sweat and the woman next to me exhales a low whistle. Doubt eclipses my excitement before it can sink in. Certainly, this is part of the game – Monopoly Money live in front of a studio audience.

"Play will begin at 10 o'clock pm, and last until 6 o'clock am. When the chime sounds the Hares may begin. The Hounds may commence pursuit thirty seconds after the chime. Play ends when the chimes sound again. Good luck."

The screens blacken, drowning us in shadows. A loud click followed by a hum sounds nearby and the overhead lights spark, flooding the room with white hot fluorescence.

I press my fingers to my eyes. "Some warning would have been nice."

Mikey hooks his thumbs into his jeans, frowning. "Doesn't this mean we're playing against each other?"

"I guess. Just act like you're chasing me and when morning comes, I'll split whatever I win with you."

"Or you could wait for me in the stairwell and I'll meet you there," he offers.

"Won't that be kind of obvious? There's no way the other teams aren't considering the same thing." I take another look at the players, huddled tightly with their partners, strategizing, planning. "It's too easy. For five million dollars there's gotta be a catch."

"For five million dollars does it matter?" He bends at the waist, reaching his fingers to his toes.

"What are you doing?"

"I'm stretching." He takes a wide step forward and lunges. "If I'm chasing you for the next eight hours, I should be limber."

I can't argue with that.

The chime tolls and the hares take off, scattering like mice caught in a pantry. A robotic voice rings over the loudspeaker, counting down from thirty. Mikey calls after me, "Remember! We are *'to strive, to seek, to find, and not to yield!'*"

27, 26, 25…

I slow to a jog and yell over my shoulder. "I don't know what that means."

"It's what we say in my LARPing group, you know, like a pep talk, Hooah etcetera."

22, 21,20…

My eye twitches. "Right." I pivot, narrowly missing the corner of an upturned filing cabinet and launch my body into the nearest door. Mikey seems like an okay guy, but I'm only now realising that I know nothing about him, nothing at all.

15, 14, 13…

I descend a dusty staircase deep into building's concrete bowels, each level blinking with a watchful red eye. I arrive at the bottom, the weight of an entire edifice above me. I push open the exit, palms leaving a sweaty residue. It's cold here, noiseless but for the occasional footstep overhead. Papers are strewn about a cracked and crumbling floor, office chairs and desks line the walls, draped carelessly with sheets gnawed into lace from rats and moths. I slow my gait and calm my breath.

Across the room a body surges through the door. I dive behind the nearest table, crouching tight to the ground, peering through tattered fabric.

It's the whistling woman from earlier. She stumbles over a cardboard box and crashes to the ground, plumes of dust ballooning over her face. Her hair is matted, face flushed with sweat. She has a cut on her left cheek, a ribbon of red dripping down her chin and onto her shirt.

I chuckle softly. She'll never make it through the night if she exhausts herself in the first half hour. I think about telling her as much, but then realize that the fewer the hares, the more money for Mikey and I. But then, doesn't that mean more money for the hounds?

The grinding of metal against metal shatters my thoughts, as the door she came through swings open. The bearded-bald man lumbers in then stops, lingering by the doorframe. His gaze settles on the woman, now clasping her ankle.

He trudges toward her and she scrambles away, pushing against the cement with her hands. For a fleeting moment I detect horror shadowing her face. I blink away the dust and refocus my eyes.

He's above her now, and she's trembling, arms raised as a shield above her head.

He kneels and wraps his arms around her head as she kicks and lashes vainly. A nauseating snap rings in my ears. He stands and brushes the dust from his knees. The trembling has ceased, body still, the room quiet.

I clamp my hand over my mouth and curl inward. I gulp back a scream fighting against the vomit lurching up my throat.

His footsteps fall, heavy and sinister; I hear the scraping of the door, and he's gone.

I release my hand and my stomach empties. I'm heaving; Purging the sickening echo of shattered bone from my body.

I unfurl my limbs and cautiously stand with the help of a table leg. I take a few tremulous steps toward her.

She can't be any older than twenty, twenty-five at the most. The cut on her cheek has smeared blood through her hair and over her throat. I gently nudge her arm with my toe, knowing already there would be no response.

Somewhere far above me I hear a scream, it's faint, smothered by layers of graded stone and cement, but it's enough for me to understand.

I race to the door and heave it open, colliding into Mikey's broad frame.

"Found you." He grins. "I thought it'd take longer."

"Fuck that. We gotta get out of here," I rasp.

"What are you talking about?" His arms fall to his sides, disappointed. "The game just started."

I point at the corpse behind me. "This isn't hide and seek. They're hunting for real. I saw it happen."

He peers over my shoulder, eyes wide. "Fuck are you joking?"

"We need to get out, maybe there's an emergency exit somewhere."

He shrugs. "We're not supposed to leave, remember?"

"Fuck the rules Mikey, we need to get out of here, we need—" And then I see it. His face is indifferent, cold. All traces of affability have bled out, eyes desiccated and cruel.

"You've played before." My throat closes around the words.

He nods. "I've played before."

Our eyes connect; I don't wait for him to move and I throw my body weight against his, slamming him against the wall. His head connects with a cinder block, and he staggers. I sprint up the stairs, taking them three at a time.

I climb four, maybe five flights before hurtling through an exit on my left. Before me is a sprawling office floor, a maze of derelict cubicles and barren conference rooms housed behind glass panels. In the opposite corner a red blinking eye gapes at me through the gloom, chronicling the theatre of horror.

I weave through the maze. My foot hooks over something solid and I stagger forward and fall, my head narrowly missing the corner of a desk. Next to me lay a body, broken and still, their face obscured by blood.

The familiar scrape of an opening door catches at my bones. My muscles contract and I lay motionless on the floor, my eyes staring into those of the dead.

I will the pounding in my ears to quiet, listening for methodical footsteps of one searching, rummaging, hunting.

Another sound, barely anything, an imperceptible trap of the imagination, hums below the footfall. The murmur rises to a moan. The moan deepens and the lips stir, eyelids fluttering.

I reach out and place a finger on their mouth. "I know it hurts," I whisper, "but you have to be quiet now."

The moan swells into a sputter, and the footsteps resume, closer now. I tighten my hand over their mouth and draw their head to my chest. "Shh... please, please, shh..."

From a gap under the desk I see the eclipse of a shadow drawing near.

The body's head is pressing into my hand now, and I press back, my fingers slick with their blood and bile. I feel them straining, quaking, desperate.

The shadow has stopped again, and I clench my eyes shut, fearing it will sense my gaze. I grip my bloody companion close to me as seconds merge into minutes.

A crash sounds in the adjacent room and the shadow carries on, its menacing footfall in pursuit. I hear the door on the opposite side of the room open and slam shut. I hold my breath, unconvinced that the hunter's departure isn't a perverse ruse to lure me into the open. By degrees, after what feels like hours, my muscles relax, and I exhale.

I slacken my grip and release my companion from my arms.

"If you don't move you might make it out." I frame their face in my hands. "Do you hear me?" Their lips are still, eyes dim. I grip their shoulders and start shaking. "Hey, you need to wake up." Their head lolls back and forth. I rest my ear against their chest, touching my fingers to their neck. I've never taken a pulse before, never checked for a heartbeat.

Never heard a silence so loud.

I lift their shoulders and slam them against the concrete, splintering my conscience into slivers of white-hot rage.

Standing, I regard the pulpy mess at my feet, oozing toward my canvas shoes. Another scream stabs at the walls, and I run for the door, swerving between partitions and cubicles.

I pass through deserted floor after deserted floor, barren but for rusting industrial equipment and the occasional hound hunched malevolently over a hare. I tread through rivulets of crimson seeping over tile, searching floor by floor.

An office door at the end of a particularly mouldy hallway clicks shut behind me as I inch closer to the ground level. Something shifts to my left and I duck, narrowly missing a collision with an iron bar from some machine or another. I dive headlong into Mikey's stomach, propelling us both to the floor.

He loses his grip on the bar and it spirals out of reach. "I'm trying to make this quick for both of us," he huffs.

I reach for the weapon and he latches onto my leg, twisting my knee. I kick wildly with my other leg, my heel landing solidly on his nose with a crack. He screams, blood running into his eyes.

My fingers wrap around the bar and I raise it over my head, pitching it against his skull. I raise it again, and let it fall. Raise it, let it fall.

Raise it, let it fall.

My hands are greased with his blood and the bar slips from my fingers, clanging to the ground.

I stand over the corpse, daring it to move.

The throbbing in my knee slashes through the panic, and gradually the frenzy subsides. I see Mikey, not through the wild eyes of horror, but with clarity spawned by catharsis. Overhead a chime rings out. The hound is dead, the hare lives on.

I limp back to the room where we started, cradling my arms across my torso. The screens blaze to life, those remaining huddled before them. Some with faces distorted with horror, others alight with triumph. The masked figure who welcomed us then, praises us now.

"Congratulations on winning tonight's event." The screens cut back to the pallet. "You have successfully completed your objective. Should you wish to accept payment, please remain here until after the presentation."

I exhale. It will be enough to quit, to disappear, to start over, to forget.

"However," the mask continues, "Should you wish to double your earnings, all are invited to next month's event as hounds, on the condition that you bring a hare. Those wishing to participate next month are dismissed."

The remnants divide. The bearded-bald man lights a cigarette and strolls to the exit, followed by several others. I look down at my torn and bloodied clothes, then back to the pallet pulsating on the screens. I think about the water stain on my ceiling. There is no nausea, no horror, only vestiges of the dead on my hands. I turn from the screen, limp across the room, down the hallway, and into the morning sun.

There is a room, not one room, but thousands scattered across the globe, and in each room sits a person, not one person but thousands, hunched over keyboards, mouses clicking, awash in the electric light of monitors.

The rooms are musty, bloated with the tang of stale fluids and anticipation. All night they've been watching, screaming, relishing, and now the time has come to collect. A face crystalizes; venetian-masked in monochrome-white, their voice garbled like a dying woodchipper.

"This evening's event has concluded. We thank you for your patronage." The camera flickers and pixilates then rights itself. "Payment for next month's event is now due."

LUST

And finally, the penguin who needs no introduction, the legendary president of our tenants' association and Terrace VII rep will dazzle us with his completely original and last-minute entry into the poetry slam.

Garycrumb Tinies
Performed by Gary the Penguin

C is for Cleo who ran out of lives
G is for Gretchen who flicked a beehive
R is for Roy who ate plastic bags
S is for Scout-Fig Fennel super into ball gags
J is for Jan who drowned in euphony
T is for Terry with the bad HPV
G is for Gary who better damn well win
J is also for Judges who still have their skin

Judges' Notes

- What?
- Is that a threat?
- Edward Gorey here, Terrace V, Percy and I can't help but notice —
- Are you trying to get us killed, Gorey?
- Hold on, speaking for myself, there's a certain eloquence to this, perhaps the best poem ever written.

Score: 5/10

YUKON GOLD

SARAH L. PRATT & ROBERT BOSE

Muttering under his breath, Solomon Black wound a frayed cargo strap around the Chief's sagging rear bumper, praying the entire back end wouldn't fall to pieces. The ancient Winnebago had seen better days. Way better days.

"Don't worry, old girl. I'm back now."

"What was that?" asked Trace, stepping out of the side door and slamming it shut behind her.

The screech of fatigued metal forced a frown and Sol replied by way of spitting a stream of orange onto the gravel shoulder and digging another dirt smeared carrot out of his shirt pocket.

"We'll be in the Tombstone Mountains in half an hour. The Chief will hold together until then."

Trace plucked a cigarette from her mass of curls, and held it out as a peace offering. He ignored her, pressing down the peeling corners of duct taped bullet holes. She lit up, directing a stream of smoke at his face. "Jesus, Sol, enough with the brooding. It's fixable. It's always fixable."

"Says you."

"Yeah, says me."

He rummaged for another cargo strap, swearing they owned at least four, and narrowed his eyes in Trace's direction.

"What?"

"What didn't you piss away over the last few months?"

Trace sat down on the folding step. "You know, I think you were happier as a gopher."

Sol munched the carrot, the recent past floating like a dream in his scrambled mind. He'd died. Sort of. Head smashed in by a giant demonic mascot in Torrington. Trace had used the relic they'd unearthed in the Badlands to transfer his soul into a taxidermied gopher. She eventually found a way to reunite him with his body and he should be appreciative. He should. Yet the cost had been high. Too damned high.

"I know that look, Solomon Black."

"You—"

"Did what I had to do."

"Maybe."

"Go ahead, list your grievances." Trace sighed. "Communication is the cornerstone of a lasting relationship."

Sol took a deep breath. "You wrecked the Chief, twice. Got the only mechanic I trust killed. Murdered a legendary Knight of Columbus and countless Vatican operatives. Burned down half of Taber along with the few bridges we had left, to the point we had flee to the fucking Yukon. I miss anything?"

"I shrunk your favourite Hawaiian shirt at the laundromat in Watson Lake."

"The orange one with the pineapples?"

Trace produced another cigarette from her hair, offering it to him. "I'm actually sorry about that."

Sol reached for the dart and stopped himself. No. The first thing he'd promised himself when Trace magicked his strangely restored body from the ether was that he'd treat it as a temple. That had been half the problem, he'd gotten soft, fallen to his vices. His many vices. Complicated shirts were one thing he couldn't quit. Trace was another. He dug another carrot from his pocket.

"I'm also sorry about your mechanic, but shit happens. The Chief will make it to Niall's place and he's the best damn tinker around these parts."

Sol stopped nibbling and stared at her. "Niall?"

"I knew you'd—"

"Apple tree Niall?"

"This is why I didn't tell you."

"Waterbed Niall?"

"Shut it."

"Old enough to be your grandpa, Niall?"

"SHUT. THE. FUCK. UP."

Laughing so hard he had to hold himself up against the side of the motorhome, Sol yowled at Trace who couldn't help laughing with him. Trace had no real shame in her game, and he loved that about her. He really did.

They rolled into the Tombstones just as the sun set low as it ever did this time of year in the North of the world. To Sol's surprise, Trace pulled out a paper map rather than her damn phone.

"You know where this place is?"

"It's been a while…" She glanced between map and road as the scenery went by in a blur of pine. "Oh! Turn here."

"Jesus!" Sol braked, cranking the wheel hard, hearing the pops and groans of the poor old Chief's chassis. They juddered down a wide-ish trail and through clacking teeth Sol asked, "Are you…sure…this is…a road?"

Trace shrugged. "It's a way."

Whatever the fuck that meant. When Trace gave an answer like that there was no point asking for clarification. Like some things couldn't be made simple enough for a blockhead like him.

Branches scoured the Chief's flanks, no doubt scraping off Sol's carefully placed duct tape. It wasn't the first time he'd considered wringing Trace's neck, and wouldn't be the last. He glanced over at his short-suffering partner in semi-profitable chaos, a thoughtful slant to her mouth, curls flying every which way, body nearly jostling right out of that little sundress. He wasn't ready to make up, but he could appreciate the view in the meantime.

Washboard turned onto sparse gravel, then a clearing occupied by a ramshackle cabin.

Sol cut the engine and cracked the window, letting in chalky mountain air and the whine of a million ravenous mosquitos. The cabin consisted of four weather-furred log walls, with smoke curling whimsically from the crumbling chimney. The veranda sagged under a salvage yard's worth of piled-up junk. Rusty iron, splintered window frames, hand tools, and old machinery from another century. Sol was so busy calculating the date of his last tetanus shot that he almost missed the rocking chair where Gandalf the Grey sat unmoving, hat low over his face, pipe in his mouth, shotgun across his lap.

"The fuck?" Sol stared through the windshield at the craggy old-timer.

Trace glared. "I told you he was older."

"He's a fossil."

"He's young at heart," Trace said, with uncharacteristic stricture in her voice. "And the only fence around that can unload this damn relic."

Sol eyed the shotgun. "He's expecting us?"

"We'll be welcome."

Sol scowled. Again, no point asking. She hopped out of the Chief and the second her feet hit the earth the wizard popped out of that chair like he was spring loaded. Flicking his hat brim above his eyes, he raised the shotgun, aiming both barrels at the Chief.

Sol braced for yet another new windshield.

Ever the death wisher, Trace stepped into the line of fire. "That how you greet a lady these days?"

The gun stayed raised but a wide white smile sliced through the thicket of steely beard.

"Darlin'!" He tossed the shotgun aside and ambled across the scrubby yard in bare feet. Trace ran into his arms and he swept her up, spinning until her damn flip-flops flew off. She wrapped her legs around the old man's waist as he grasped the back of her head pulling her in for a kiss deep enough to count as a medical procedure.

Sol grunted. What else had he expected? For such a destructive reptile, Trace maintained unusually genial relations with her formers. Sol wondered how many others she'd *reconnected* with while he was a rodent—when she wasn't busy trashing his RV, bartering his Blanton's bottle toppers, and getting his friends dead.

They were still sucking face when Sol clambered out of the driver's seat and slammed the door just a touch harder than necessary.

With a pop, Trace broke the seal between her and the old man's orifices but remained wrapped around him like a horny koala. "Hey, baby. This is my friend Niall. The legendary tinker."

"Solomon Black!" Niall exclaimed, still grinning and groping. "No introduction needed, my boy. I am an ardent admirer of your work. And your taste," he added, winking at Trace as he set her on her feet, squeezing one last handful of her ass, before extending that same hand to shake Sol's.

Niall at least had the decency to prove himself hospitable. He insisted they stay in the cabin's only bed, claiming he slept most nights in his rocking chair anyway. He then fried up three enormous steaks with wild onions and mushrooms. Maybe it was his dietary sabbatical as a gopher, but Sol had never had a better meal. And when a tumbler of bourbon was pushed into his hand, he grudgingly admitted the old Tinker was maybe not totally insufferable.

"You know the way to a girl's heart," Trace sighed, settling into the shabby sofa and patting her stomach.

"I never leave a beautiful woman unsatisfied." Niall struck a match on the stone mantel, beneath a plaque-mounted fish, and gallantly swept in, touching the flame to Trace's cigarette.

She turned to Sol, blowing a delicate smoke ring. His hand itched to rip the dart out of her grasp and suck the whole thing down in one drag. He took a long pull of whisky instead. "Niall, look…we uh…appreciate all this, but I'm sure you've gathered this isn't a social call."

Niall sat back in yet another rocking chair, retrieving a knife and a lump of wood from one of his many pockets. He began to whittle in a silence so long it could only be intentional, meaning the negotiations had begun.

"We've got something you might be interested in," Sol said.

"Aside from the obvious?" Niall's gaze travelled to Trace as he arched a bushy eyebrow.

Sol grit his teeth. He wasn't a jealous guy. Never had been and wasn't now. Not exactly. But things hadn't exactly been solid since he turned back. His irritation wasn't even about this handsome old lech. Or even Trace, really. Sol didn't know himself anymore. He was so fucking angry all the time. Twitchy. Probably PTSD or some shit from his soul being translocated, twice. And now there was a distance between them, and feeling Trace so far away made Sol feel lost.

Shavings curled at Niall's feet, filling the room with the scent of green wood as they snowed down over gnarled toenails so long Sol felt sorry for the man's shoes. He side-eyed Trace. She restrained her smile but couldn't keep it from pinching a dimple in her cheek. His skin flushed with warmth that wasn't just the bourbon. She was giving him the floor. A chance to reclaim a little more of his old self.

"Familiar with the Relic of Gerasene?" Sol asked.

Niall threw his head back in a full-throated laugh, luxurious silver and gun-metal mane cascading down his back. "Now that's one I haven't heard before. But if what you have is worth anything at all, I guarantee top dollar."

Trace reached into her enormous handbag and pulled out a clay disc, clapping it down on the table. "It's the real deal."

"Darlin' I don't doubt you believe it. But without authentication it's not worth much but a few clams to an unscrupulous archaeologist."

Sol frowned. "If you're familiar with our work you ought to know we don't deal in fakes."

A log popped in the fire, ejecting a glowing nugget onto the rag rug in front of the hearth. Niall stood and ground it out with one thickly calloused heel. "Assuming it's legitimate, you ought to know it's an impossible fence. I'm truly sorry, Solomon. Best case, I find a collector interested in an artifact, that while imbued with colorful mythology, is ultimately just an ancient ashtray."

Trace removed a wad of black cloth from her handbag and Sol's memory chimed. He'd seen it before.

"I knew you'd want proof," Trace said. "Fortunately, I managed to snag the world's most incompetent adorcist's six-demon-bag before he could entirely empty it into an army of stuffed rodents."

"Are you serious?" Sol choked.

Niall's blade and toothy smile gleamed in the firelight.

"You've been hoarding a demon?" Sol gestured to the sack, sloshing a good amount of bourbon out of his glass. "And you never thought to tell me?"

Trace nailed him with a look utterly void of her usual humour. "Don't even go there."

Sol moved to clutch the crucifix he no longer wore around his neck. The revelation that he'd once been a priest, a member of the Dirty Bishop's order no less, had come as something of a shock to Trace. They hadn't had time to discuss it, since Sol was more or less immediately tossed into a gopher himself.

"Show me what you got, Darlin'."

Trace gave the old man a smile sweeter than any she'd bestowed on Sol in recent memory. "I could give you incantations and a light show, but that's just garnish, it's the relic doing the heavy lifting here." She opened the sack in the general direction of the clay disc and said, "*Expurgefacio*."

The disc didn't so much as rattle.

"That it?" Niall asked.

"Wait," Sol said.

"For what?" barked a gravelly voice. "Hell to freeze up tighter than a righteous nun?"

"It worked!" Trace clapped her hands. "Only my second time, you know."

"Second time's the best, sister. You get to do the weird stuff..." The mounted fish above the fireplace wriggled in wall-eyed consternation. "Speaking of weird, where the fuck am I? And why can't I move?"

Sol's heart trip-hammered, and his throat swelled at the memory of that trapped, tight darkness. Feeling his soul crushed and crammed into something dirty and dead. Bourbon surged up his esophagus and he swallowed hard.

"It's okay, baby," Trace said softly, laying her hand on his tattooed arm. He jerked away. What would she know of okay? She's the one who did it to him.

"If it's not too much trouble," the fish drawled. "Could I impose on one of you useless assholes for a mirror?"

Trace retrieved a compact from her bag and bounced to the mantel, holding it in front of the reanimated fish. Its mouth managed to dilate even wider as a choking sob erupted in its throat. "You gotta be shitting me."

"Best I could do, friend." Trace turned and sauntered over to Niall. There was something odd about the way she stood, hip cocked, the fire at her back, and Niall's shadow stretching almost all the way to the door. But Sol couldn't put his finger on it.

"An impossible fence, yeah?" she said.

"I may have spoken too soon," Niall admitted.

"Ya think?" the fish said. "I spend the last thirty years in a fuckin' bag only to end up in a fish, and for what? Some shitty demo? My forever home was supposed to be a sweet blonde with big fat titties. You got some balls, bitch. Stealing my destiny."

Trace ignored the foul-mouthed flounder, narrowing her eyes at Niall. "We have a deal or what?"

"You do at that, Darlin'." Niall reached out, curling a shop-hardened hand around the back of Trace's knee, sliding it up her thigh. "On one condition."

Sol sighed. "Seriously dude, I'm right here."

Niall chuckled, withdrawing his paw. "In that regard my affections are unconditional. No, I'm proposing a trade. I scratch your back, you scratch mine."

"No one is scratching your anything, pal."

"It's a bit of a yarn, a bedtime story if you will."

"Pass."

Trace threw her hands up. "Hear the man out, Sol. Jesus."

"Yeah, *Sol*," the fish said. "I wanna hear the fuckin' story."

Sol sat back, seething.

Niall stroked his beard, leaving shavings in the foliage. "There's an abandoned mine nearby. Known only to a few locals. Lore tells of a large cache of gold inside, just waiting for an intrepid soul to march in and take it, yet no one ever has."

"Fuck sakes…" Sol muttered. "I supposed it's cursed?"

"Haunted," Niall corrected.

Flames danced in Trace's eyes. "By what?"

Niall shrugged. "Boobytraps most likely, as it's quite true that no one who has ventured in has ever ventured out again. Happened enough that folks stopped talking about it, and as years passed most of them forgot. Intentionally, I suspect."

"Hehe…boobies," grunted the fish.

"I take it you've never tried?" Sol asked.

Niall's blade shook slightly as he tucked it and his bird in progress into his pocket. "While young at heart, I'm not spry of limb enough to go tucking and rolling down a mineshaft. Strapping lad like you, on the other hand…" Niall gave Sol an earthy onceover that made him blush "And then there's the ghosts. All in all, I'd simply prefer not to."

"I don't believe in ghosts, old man—"

Trace scoffed. The fish rolled its glass eyes.

"But I do believe in gold," Sol continued. "I'll check out this mine, but we split the take even and you fix up the Chief while I'm at it."

"Deal!" Niall lunged in and clapped his massive hand into Sol's while reaching for the bottle of bourbon. "Let's drink to it."

Sol jolted from a dark dream. The same damn dream every night since his translocation. Burrowing under a vengeful farmer's field, fleeing a tidal wave of water pumped into the network of tunnels he called home, but no matter how fast he dug, or where he eventually popped out, his only reward was a bullet through his spine.

Sol shuddered and extracted the arm wrapping a softly snoring Trace. He heaved himself off the waterbed, smeared the bourbon crusts from his eyes, and with full light spearing the slit between the blackout curtains, checked his watch. 5 a.m. Land of the midnight sun. Better than the winter at least, when it was dark twenty-three hours a day.

A tin of coffee perched on a counter stacked with hand-carved Ouija boards. Niall did have a knack, Sol admitted. He heated water in a beat-up kettle, chugged down some surprisingly tasty coffee, and ducked out the back door.

Or tried to.

"Nothing like morning wood," the fish crowed, tapping his head against his plaque.

"Shh," Sol hissed. "Go back to sleep."

"Goddamn, you two are boring," the thing moaned, "An honest to hell waterbed and you can't be bothered to make a few waves? I sense tension, and not the good kind."

Sol eyed the lever action 30-30 leaning in one junk strewn corner. Might come in handy. Though the noise would wake the dead and probably wouldn't do much to quiet the demon even if he blew it's head off. "Shut it, fish face."

"I have a name, you know."

"Yeah?"

"Barthamus the Butcher of —"

"Right, every one of you pests is the Butcher of someone or some place."

"I happen to be named in the early Old Testament."

"If it's one thing I do know it's the Bible and you're not in it. You're also not in the Lesser Key of Solomon, so you ain't shit."

"Ever heard of an alias? Not telling anyone my *true* name"

"Blah, blah, blah, nobody cares, Bart. I got work to do."

"Smoke me a kipper, you're an idiot. Do you even know where you're going?"

Sol paused. Did he? Best to kill two birds with one fish. He wrenched the plaque from the wall, tucked the bulky thing under an arm, found a flashlight big enough to be used as a truncheon, and padded out into the junkyard.

"Lead on, Mcduff."

"That's misquote, you know. It's actually 'Lay on, Macduff.'"

"Okay, fish. I see we have a failure to communicate here." Sol held the plaque so his eye was an inch from the demon's. "Can the mouthy crap. Now. Or I swear to God, I'll get Trace to stuff you into Niall's toenails."

Bart strained against the pegs pinning him to the board. "You're a monster, Sol. A monster."

"Don't you know it. Now, *fish*, make yourself useful and tell me where this blasted mine is."

They followed a mile of overgrown double-track through mosquito infested muskeg leading to a rocky spur of a small mountain. A semi-collapsed wooden building thrust mossy ribs to the sky and an old rockfall choked what appeared to be half a dozen collapsed cave entrances. In the center of the clearing gaped a black hole big enough to swallow a car. Two long beams spanned the hole. Rusty mining equipment poked from clumps of scrub grass.

"Blasted mine, oh priestly one."

Sol tossed the fish to the ground, and peered into the hole

"It goes all the way down; in case you were wondering."

"There's running water, I'm guessing seventy or eighty feet below us."

"Bullshittery," said the fish. "Like you can know that."

"I can smell it. This looks like the only way in," Sol wandered over to the disintegrating structure, wrenched open a splintered door and half the wall crumpled, expelling a cloud of dust, mold, and the faint odour of rotting animal. He tore away the debris, finding a tattered nylon tarp, and under it…

"What did you find, bullet head?" asked the fish.

"Dead guy."

A local, Sol decided, based on the denim work pants and red flannel. The corpse was little more than chewed up bones and desiccated skin. Sprawled face down, a bulging canvas pack askew on his back. Sol flipped him over. A small wooden bird on a copper chain looped the man's neck and Sol worked it free. Nothing in any of the crusty pockets. The guy's arms were unbending sticks, so Sol snapped them with his boot, tugged off the pack and walked back to where Bart's scales glinted in the morning sun.

"And?" Bart asked, staring into the sky. "I can't see shit like this, you know."

Sol dangled the carved bird above the demon. "Look familiar."

"Another one of the Tinker's dimwit envoys."

"Looks like a wild animal, or several wild animals. Chewed him up something fierce." Sol searched the pack. A coil of climbing rope. Two ascenders in reasonably good shape. A prospectors hammer. Flares, matches, and a first-aid kit.

"You really believe Niall never came scavenging here?"

"Got the feeling he's scared shitless of this place," Sol said. Church doctrine was vague on the concept of ghosts. If they existed in any form, scholars believed they were associated with Purgatory, another vague concept. Sol had seen a lot of crazy things, never ghosts though. He jammed Bart's plaque into the webbing criss-crossing the back of the pack and shrugged it over his shoulders. "And away we go. Unless, of course, you'd rather stay here. I'm sure whatever chewed up that stiff is long gone. Racoons don't like fish, do they?"

"No, no," sputtered the demon. "You need all the help you can get. And whatever you *believe*, you don't know shit about ghosts, which I assure you are real. Real as demons."

Exactly what a bag demon would say. Tricksters, every last one of them. Sol tested the beams spanning the hole, finding them sturdy. He threaded the rope through his legs and around his waist, knotted the end around the beam, and began his descent. The reinforced shaft had obviously been constructed to lower and raise a small platform. Sol lowered himself into the sharp mineral smell and roar of rushing ground water as the shaft opened into a cavern bisected by a stream spraying from a vertical crack in one wall. It crashed into the floor, then plunged off into an enormous chasm Sol's light didn't make a dent in.

"All the way down," said the fish.

Sol shone his light along the ledge they were on, which curled its way under the mountain, ending at a hole in the rock face. Twenty feet down this natural stream channel, a cave-in blocked his way. Sol paused, munching on a carrot.

"So, wanna talk about it?" the fish whispered.

"It?"

"It's rough, the translocation. Eleven times now for me and I gotta say it doesn't get easier. Though the first sucked the most. Want to hear about it?"

"No."

"There I was, minding my own business as the best henna artist in Amenophis III's harem when *bam*, some crazed rival ejects me into a toad. Me! A common Nile toad for decades. Can you believe it? I still dream of eating bugs. You've had the dreams, right? Host memories."

Sol pried at one of the larger, linchpin rocks. It didn't budge and he moved onto the next. He didn't want to think about his months as a gopher. Or the dreams…echoes of an alternate life. Echoes that gnawed at his sanity. Sol thought he knew himself pretty well after a half century of life, yet now… He absently dug into his pocket for a carrot.

"Of course, there's lots of other things to talk about," said Bart. "Like your missy. Bent as a fucked-up slinky. Makes some seriously suspect deals."

"Old news, fish," grunted Sol, finally prying out a chunk of quartzite and backing up a step when the pile shifted. "And what would you know about it?"

"I know she's not all there, but I guess you didn't notice."

"Notice wha—"

With a grinding boom, one edge of the ceiling collapsed, forcing Sol's retreat down the tunnel, cursing. When the dust cleared, he saw that a hole now gaped open above. He wormed his way up, popping out into a timber reinforced mine tunnel.

"I love a good shaft," barked the demon.

"You're an expert miner too, I suppose." Sol shone his light in both directions, catching a glint of something in the direction he thought the mine encampment had to be. "Your second soul swap was into a canary?"

"Must you be such a withered dick? Word of mouth goes a long way in this business. One word to Mephistopheles and—"

"Jesus. How long were you in that bag, you moron? We got Meph on speed dial."

The demon stopped talking.

Sol walked towards the glint, saw it was a slice of sun coming through some camouflage netting draped across a pile of branches and junk and rocks blocking the passage. He cleared enough away to see the far edge of the clearing where they'd arrived a couple hours earlier. Dammit. If someone was trying to hide their gold, of course they'd disguise their preferred entrance. Sol should have known. Finding shit was his talent, not pissing around in the dark wet.

He returned to the wormhole he'd crawled up, noticing the rubble strewn floor gave a little. A wooden underlay? Odd. Exceptionally odd. His light pierced the gloom in the other direction, and he could make out something squarish in the distance. He took a step towards it and stopped when he felt a whisper in his ear.

"If you can't keep your trout-hole shut, at least speak up," grumbled Sol.

"That wasn't me, dipshit."

The whispering continued. Lyrical, almost musical. Sol strained, hearing a hushed word here, a muffled note there.

"There's your ghosts."

"More likely the radio. I bet the posse is up and looking for us." Sol picked his way over the rubble and felt a crunch underfoot. The unmistakable sound of snapping bone. He swept the fallen debris away to reveal a crushed ribcage. More clearing revealed two entire outstretched skeletons. Skulls shattered. Pickaxes embedded in their chests. He eyed the walls, noticed a series of concealed narrow slits. That bounce in the floor must be pressure sensor plates. "Guess Niall was right about the boobytraps."

"I'd rather find actual boobies."

"For once we agree."

With the whispers fading in and out, Sol crawled down the tunnel, gratified to hear clicks and feel the whoosh as two more sets of pickaxes whirled overhead to clang against the walls and crash down beside him. Easy, peasy. This was amateur.

More buried skeletons lay beyond. These crushed from a weight from above. Sol found the trigger plate, disabled it, and slid beyond. Next, a length of fine chain stretched across the passageway three inches above the floor. A tripwire. Hard to see in the dark if you weren't looking for it. Sol carefully stepped over, pushing through a particularly thick and dusty spiderweb complete with a thick and dusty spider. Dusty spider… Too late he realized his mistake and heard a click. A fiery glow hissed and shot away down the tunnel. A god damned fuse.

"Fuck," Sol spat, barreling after it like an enraged bull at a Spanish street festival. The fuse snaked up a wall and towards a box strapped against a ceiling beam, and with an ungainly leap, Sol got one step ahead and yanked it from its connection. He lay face down, wheezing grit and drooling carrot juice, wondering if he was indeed too old for this shit.

"Honey, we're home," said Bart in falsetto.

Sol rolled and saw a wooden pallet stacked with boxes, secured with hemp rope. The whispers were louder. Had to be a radio somewhere, playing a song.

The midnight sun betrayed no one
And never a single note was sung

"Sol, old buddy, we gotta go. Now."

Dragging himself to his feet, Sol dusted off one of the boxes, dug out his butterfly knife, cut the bindings, and levered it open. The inside glittered with gold nuggets ranging from grains of sand to as big as his thumb. He reached for one and felt a cold draft against his hand.

"Don't, you idiot, can't you see them?"

"You're paranoid." Sol grabbed the largest nugget of the lot and screamed when teeth fastened on his leg.

"The hells happened to you?" Trace demanded when Sol staggered back onto the cabin's front porch.

The fish cackled behind his back. "Your defrocked fella is now a touch more open-minded on the existence of ghosts."

Sol grimaced. "Whatever they were, they swarmed me."

"Serves you right, sneaking off like a rodent." Trace said, rummaging in her bag and pulling out a small first aid kit. She then shoved Sol into Niall's outside rocking chair and dropped to her knees, poking and prodding through his shredded jeans at the bloody gouges in his legs. "There's at least fifty bites here. You're gonna need a whack of stitches. And a rabies shot."

"Thought I'd do some recon is all." He winced as she swabbed his legs with some potion smelling of oregano and Everclear.

"Could've left a fucking note," she said as she popped the suture needle through a flap of skin, yanking a length of nylon gut with it. "I could've gone with Niall for a night on the town, yet here I am, sewing up your sorry ass as always."

He watched the hard crease of her brow as she focused on her doctoring. Trace was a healer at heart, though she'd rip the heart out of anyone who dared accuse her of such tenderness. And since when did she not look Sol in the eye while giving him hell?

Sol extended a hand to stroke her hair but held back. Something was wrong. Bart said she wasn't all there. But she seemed whole as ever as she knelt in front of him, embroidering his skin, the low sun stretching the rocking chair's shadow across the porch. Sol was the fragmented one. Why bother bringing him back when no amount of stitches could hold him together?

Just then Niall rounded the corner of the cabin. "Well, darlin', I happened to have some Winnebago scrap, and I got your rig patched up near as new—" His gregarious grin froze when he spotted Sol in his rocking chair.

"Surprised?" Sol drawled with a grin of his own, pulling the copper chain out of his pocket and letting the carved owl dangle between them. "Seems I'm not the first you've sent in there to die. Am I, old man?"

Niall boomed with laughter and bounded onto the porch, clapping Sol hard on the shoulder. "Don't look at me that way, son. I made 'em all the same deal I made you. They didn't hold up their end of the bargain."

The fish cocked his dried out little head. "Like you weren't setting my good pal up, you old fuck. He never woulda made it without my help."

"We're not pals," Sol snapped. "The only help I need from you is to keep your slimy gob shut."

"That's not what your what your mom said."

Trace flicked the fish hard in the gills. "I will translocate your nasty ass back in that bag you little shit."

"Okay, okay," Bart cringed. "Too far."

Trace arched an eyebrow.

Bart sighed. "Solomon, I apologize for besmirching your sainted mother. Mea Culpa."

Sol turned to Niall. "You weren't lying about the gold though."

A gleam shone in Niall's eye. "Honestly, I never knew for certain. You sure?"

"Pretty sure." Sol reached into his pocket pulling out a golf ball-sized nugget. "Lot more where that came from."

"And the traps?" Niall asked.

"Disabled," Sol said. "Your red shirts were nice enough to alert me to most of them. The gold isn't even hard to get to. It's just…"

"The ghosts," Trace said, knotting the last stitch and muttering some unintelligible incantation. "Start talking, Niall. What exactly do you know about these ectoplasmic ankle biters?"

Niall drew a long breath.

"Wait!" Bart yapped, pausing, going crossed-eyed. "The song, the song in the mine. I know it…or, the fish does, hang on…" Bart cleared his brittle throat and sang an off-key scale up and down before launching into song.

There once was a mine that shone with gold
Though around it a grim dark legend is told
Nine girls in gowns and ribbons and curls
Rose from their beds and fled

Song of the missing mine girls
Who died in their gowns and ribbons and curls
Called by the greed of men
To guard their hidden gold

The midnight sun betrayed no one
And never a single note was sung
The girls walked silent to the mine
And vanished down below

Song of the missing mine girls
Who died in their gowns and ribbons and curls
Called by the greed of men —

"Right, I think we've got it," Trace interrupted, wincing at the discordant tune resonating in the mountain air. "You're saying this is more than a simple haunt?"

The fish chuckled. "I'm saying nine little girls in their nighties just piranha'd your hubby."

"We're not married," they retorted in unison.

"Well pardon the fuck outta me," Bart said. "Figured a former man of the cloth woulda made an honest woman out of you by now."

Trace gave Sol a look he couldn't decipher before turning to Niall. "So is that it? Any other surprises we should know about?"

Niall nodded. "That's the long and short of it. You know, pirates used to kill a man and bury him atop their treasure. Rightly figuring most folks stop digging when they hit a body."

"This is next level," said Trace. "Whoever stashed that gold wasn't content to protect it with mere boobytraps."

Sol regarded the mess of stitched up smiles adorning his skin. "So they killed a bunch of kids? That's cold."

"Fucked up," Bart agreed.

Trace shrugged. "But not especially difficult. Basic summoning spell and you've got yourself an army of kindergartners sleepwalking all the way down a mineshaft. Fortunately," she reached into her bag, pulling out one of her many battered notebooks, "I've got the know-how to blast those little ghouls out of that mine for good."

Niall clapped his hands. "Hot damn! We got a way in. What are we sitting around jawing for?"

Trace cocked her head. "What's all this *we*?"

Niall paused mid-jig.

Sol could only feel sorry for Niall even as his own heart leapt high as it had the day he first set eyes on Trace, in the process of nicking a book from a private occult library in Beverly Hills. The woman had many talents but negotiation was not one of them. Meaning she didn't. And if she did, even odds the dupe wouldn't live long enough to collect their share of the spoils. Niall was bleeding into shark infested waters and Sol was here for it. He rocked back in the chair and wished for a tub of popcorn.

"Ruthless as she is beautiful," Niall said crouching down and stroking Trace's cheek with a callused thumb. "Perhaps fifty-fifty is no longer appropriate compensation. Sixty-forty?"

Trace smiled. "Here's the thing. Sol knows where the gold is. Necromancy is quite honestly below my paygrade, and I'm just not seeing what you bring to the table, old man."

Niall changed course, realizing charm wouldn't grease his way out of this. "The relic. There's no one else who can offload it for you."

Trace blew an errant curl off her forehead. "Think I might hang on to it. Could come in handy."

"Find me an upgrade?" Bart piped up. "Nothing fancy, I'm thinking house cat."

Cool wind cut through the golden evening as Sol observed Niall scanning the porch for defensive weapons and exit strategies. Trace sat patiently at Sol's feet, allowing it. A healer by nature, but she'd just as willingly kill if it suited her purposes. Machiavelli had nothing on Trace. Much as he wouldn't mind seeing her pull a knife from her hair and jam it into the tinker's throat, Sol knew it wasn't right. Niall was an old man. A gigantic perv. But he had fixed the Chief. And there was no fucking way they were keeping that relic.

"Eighty-twenty," Sol said. "And that's us being honourable."

Niall relaxed as he whistled and pulled a now laughing Trace to her feet and into his arms like a doll. Sol didn't even hate it. The way she played the game was something to behold.

"Darlin' you drive a hard bargain," Niall said, dipping his head for a kiss she gracefully deflected.

"Thanks, *darlin'*," Sol said. "Now, do you have a winch somewhere in that junkyard?"

It was nearing midnight but the sun remained a golden glow through the Tombstone mountains. Sol had to admit the tinker had done a bang-up job. The Chief looked great with her new body panels, purred like a cheetah with a freshly tuned engine. Sol backed the motorhome up to the mine while Trace and Niall gave him direction from the rear.

"All good, babe!" Trace called.

Sol cut the engine and hopped out. Trace and Niall stood by the winch bolted onto the trailer hitch.

"Hey!" Bart hollered from inside the Chief. "Don't forget me!"

"Why did we bring him?" Trace asked.

Sol shrugged. "Little grouper is growing on me."

Niall unspooled the cable a few feet. "Guess you and the Mrs'll go in, vaporize the ghosties, hook up to the gold and I can pull it on out?"

"We're not married," Trace said. "I'll go in and deal with the ghosts. And then I'll drive while you earn your twenty percent helping Sol."

Sol wasn't fussy over who did what. He was just overjoyed that something was going to actually work for a change. Even without the proceeds from the relic, that gold was enough money to…to do anything. Fix their countless legal transgressions. Take a vacation. Retire in some non-extradition country. As soon as they divvied up the nuggets, Sol would take Trace to the most expensive hotel in Dawson City, order up a sour toe cocktail, then they'd head up to their room and over a bottle of bourbon and some broken furniture, things would get right between them. One way or another.

Sol retrieved Bart from the Chief.

"Thanks, brother."

"Don't mention it," Sol replied, too buzzed on optimism to even correct the stupid reptile.

He wandered back to where Trace and Niall were arguing the finer details of cable tension while pelican-sized mosquitoes buzzed around his head. The sun's rays slid almost parallel over the earth, smearing the Chief's and Niall's shadow into the forest. Sol glanced down, where indeed his own shadow pulled like taffy to the east.

They all had shadows. All but one.

"Told you she wasn't all there," Bart said, sounding truly sympathetic.

The fish squawked as Sol dropped him to the ground and marched over to Trace, grabbing her shoulders and spinning her to face him. "What did you do?"

"Settle down," she laughed. "The show hasn't even started yet."

"Who'd you give it to? What kind of deals were you making while I was gone?" He shook her hard enough to make her teeth clack.

Niall edged forward. "No need to get hands on."

Trace wrenched out of Sol's grip with a venomous snarl. "What are you talking about?"

"Don't play dumb. Your shadow Trace, or rather your entire lack of same?"

She seemed genuinely surprised. "Oh…right."

"You fucking forgot you sold your soul?"

"Don't be so dramatic. I was in a jam. Meph offered to help me out…in exchange for a memory. The shadow should grow back. Mostly."

"What did you let him take?"

"How the fuck should I know? That's kinda the whole point of cutting out a memory."

Sol raked his nails over his shaved skull. "We don't make those kinds of deals, Trace. Not ever.

Souls don't grow back. And why didn't you tell me? How could you keep that from me?"

"Oh," she stepped back, fire all but shooting from her tongue. "You wanna talk about keeping secrets, motherfucker? Or should I say *Father* Motherfucker?"

Niall cleared his throat. "I'm going to mosey into the trees for a smoke and give you two a spot of privacy."

"Yeah, you do that, Niall," Sol sneered.

Niall winked at Trace. "Should you need a shoulder to cry on…"

Trace regarded him with stony silence. He got the hint and tromped off in a sweet cloud of pipe tobacco.

Sol exhaled and made an effort to lower his voice. "I always meant to tell you, but there never seemed to be a good time and then I realized how much it would hurt you and…besides it's in the —"

"In the past?" She shook her head in disgust. "Well tell me, *Father*. Exactly how far back does the statute of limitations go? Or are you going to be honest and admit there's different rules for you than me. At least now I know why the Dirty Bishop hates me so much. I stole his boyfriend."

"For Christ's Sake," he groaned and then gasped as her open hand cracked him hard across the ear.

"You were a priest, Sol!" she shrieked. "Serving the literal source of all rot in the modern world. You took orders from the assholes that force women to give birth, rape their children, steal from the poor, fuel wars and tyranny, and burn people like me at the stake, all the while sitting on their mountain of treasure like untouchable fucking dragons."

Sol felt every word like a bullet to the chest. "Why do you think I left?"

"I don't know who you are anymore." Her eyes simmered with tears. "And still, everything I've done the last year has been for you."

"Bullshit," he said. "Turning me into a gopher was the best vacation you ever had. Like you weren't having the time of your life blowing up Vatican goons. Keeping a demon stowaway and evidently selling shreds of your soul—the one God Damned thing we swore we'd never do.

Trace stepped back and gazed long and hard into dark mouth of the mine. "I don't remember the first ten years of my life."

"What?" he asked, taken aback by her segue.

"Yeah," she said. "Whatever happened before I was found…it's gone. I don't have a childhood. Parents, siblings, school. Fucking church even. Maybe? It's a blank. And that's why I remember everything since. Every single thing. I don't much care about whatever shred of my soul Meph gobbled up. But you're the only soul in existence that I would give up a memory for, Solomon Black."

They were at an impasse. He wanted to hold her. He wanted to murder her. He wanted to lecture and rail and teach her a lesson. Except she was right. But that didn't mean he was wrong, and he wasn't ready to let that go.

Sol joined her in gazing into the darkness of the mine. "Are we doing this or not?"

"Let's banish these bitches," she said, digging a crusty grimoire from the sack she called a purse. She thumbed to a marked page, and pushed her way through the camo netting and debris they'd pulled aside. "Shouldn't take but a minute." She paused and looked back at him, eyes smoldering in the shadows. "Plenty of time for you to apologize later."

Bart whistled, a horrible dry rattle, as Trace disappeared into the mine.

"Suppose you got something to say?" Sol snatched the fish up from the pine needle carpeted ground, leaning him against the Chief's wheel well. "Let's hear it then."

"How in all the hells did you end up with that?" Bart said.

Sol wasn't sure if he was referring to the Chief or to Trace. "Long story."

"Catch me up some time, but unless you're looking at cutting it short, you'd better go after her."

"What, now?"

"Yeah now, numb nuts. What if she gets eaten by those things? You really wanna leave it like this? I've been in love too, ya know. And you never wait until after the battle to make up. Jesus. Is this your first day? Do I gotta hold your goddamn hand through everything?"

Sol thought about it. He'd always been taught to walk away before he lost his temper. Take time to cool off. In a perfect world there'd always be time.

Niall was still off in the woods. Sol eyed the entrance to the mine.

"Take me with you," Bart said. "You're gonna need my ongoing assistance here."

They crept down the tunnel, Bart wheezing against Sol's neck. "Could you not?" he said. "That's disgusting."

Bart cleared his dusty throat. "Hear that?"

Sol listened. A faint song filtered up from the depths of the mine shaft. But it wasn't the same as before. He tucked into a hollow and spotted Trace perched atop the pallet of gold, singing softly in a language he didn't recognize. In a voice he didn't recognize. A blue halo surrounded her, filtering out to the darkness where it illuminated the ghostly outlines of nine little ones curiously gathered at the edge of the shadows, drawn in by Trace's song, they approached slowly, cautiously, hems of their nightgowns drifting above skinny ankles and bare feet, as though helpless lambs rather than giggling hellcats, capable of chewing a man's legs clean off.

Trace continued singing and the spectral children drew closer.

"Oh," Bart whispered. "This is a good one."

"You know the song?"

"Slavic lullaby. About a witch in the woods who steals wakeful rug rats and throws 'em in her stew pot."

"That's a *lullaby*?"

"Oh yeah. From the Old Country, before all this sweet dreams BS, where you scared your kids to sleep and they fuckin' loved it."

Sol listened to the lyrics drifting so naturally from Trace's mouth. This wasn't a recitation. She knew this language, like she'd spoken it from birth. He wondered if she had any recollection of learning it.

At any moment Sol expected flames and thundering commands of You Shall Not Pass. Standard ghostbusting theatre. But Trace just kept singing, and the girls crept closer, crawling on the pallet all around her, snuggling into her lap, their chubby hands twisting in her curls, arms winding around her neck, wrapping their little bodies around her limbs. All the while she sang, patting their heads and stroking their cheeks until one by one the missing mine girls lay down their heads, closed their eyes, and disappeared.

"What just happened?" Sol whispered.

"Some dickhead lured those babes from their beds," Bart said, almost solemnly. "And your girl just tucked them back in."

Sol nodded, unable to find words.

"Ever thought about having kids?" Bart asked.

Trace's head snapped up and the blue glow vanished.

"You're about as sneaky as a buffalo in bomb factory," she said in the darkness and Sol's shoulders unwound at the warmth in her voice. "What say we grab this gold and get the hell out of here? Just give me a few minutes to tidy up."

"Seems to me," said Bart from where Sol wedged him among a heap of mine tailings, "that you possess the charm of a feral hog. Did I mention I was once an advisor to Vatsyayana? Helped him transcribe the Nyaya Sutras, Siddhartha Gautama being a buddy of mine from olden times. Course

Vats was clueless." The fish tittered to himself. "Talked the talk but didn't walk the walk, if you know what I mean. Meditated, a lot. Solo. Want my advice?"

"Nope." Sol paced across the mine entrance.

"I make woodcuts of the Kama Sutra," kicked in Niall. "With some gnarly bonus positions I guarantee you've never heard of. Though," he grinned through his silver-shot thicket, "Trace probably has, the wildcat has an entire orchard of moves. Start with the Tinker's Tantalizing Tingle and progress to Niall's Naughty Nugging and she'll forget she hates your stinking guts. I'll throw in a set, gratis."

"Any boobies?" asked the demon.

"Acres."

"Sol, the old fucker is possibly right, you gotta show her the love. Squeeze out those lemons you sucked up your ass."

"What are you morons droning about now?" Trace stepped into the sun, an enveloping cloud of ethereal mist burning away in pops and sparkles.

Sol stopped pacing. "Relationship advice from Tweedle Dumb and Dumber. They should start a podcast."

Trace snorted. "The girls are snug as a bug in a rug. Have at it, lemonhead."

Heaving a glare at Bart, Sol grabbed the end of the winch cable and started dragging. "Make sure it doesn't bind or snag, I'll yell when I have it sorted." The cable played out smooth and Sol plodded back through the tunnel, past the spent traps, wincing when bones snapped and crackled under his feet. He stopped, listened, sniffed. Silence, and a hint in the air that hadn't been there before. Burnt ozone. The pallet appeared ghostless and he reached out, hand trembling, to reseal the box he'd levered open. When nothing untoward occurred, he let out the breath he'd been holding and got to work securing the cable around and through the web of hemp straps.

His bellow of "secure" echoed down the shaft and he heard Niall relay this to Trace. The cable grew taut and with a raspy groan the pallet twisted, tearing from the patch of ground it had grown into and began sliding forward in fits and jerks.

"As good as gold?" Niall hollered, his form a spindly blot across the tunnel mouth.

"Slow it down a mite."

"Roger, roger."

The pace of the pallet slackened a touch, giving Sol time to kick the moldering remains and the remnants of booby traps out of the way. Smooth sailing for a fucking change. He could almost taste that sour toe cocktail. He'd make Trace drink one too. And she would. She'd gulp it down, give him the evil eye. Order a second, a third. Showing him she could play the game. They'd fight. Make up. They always had, though this time… the void was cold and deep. He never liked secrets, hated them truth be told. His. Hers. Lot more where that came from, he knew it in his heart.

The entrance loomed near, Niall's face resembling a mischievous goblin where his nose poked through the camo netting. Fifteen feet. Ten. And with a grinding shriek, the ground beneath his feet gave way and he watched in slo-mo horror as the pallet disappeared into a widening hole, slamming into the side of a vertical shaft and mushing Sol's legs between wood and stone. A scream caught in his throat, and he choked it down, seeing stars in the half-light as falling debris pelted him. He clung, dazed, to the hemp straps, until a light from above speared his eyes.

Niall shouted from a dozen feet above. "You okay, sonny boy?"

"Do I look fucking okay?" rasped Sol, wriggling his crushed legs from beneath the pallet. "Pull us up before something comes apart." The cable had slid up off the pallet proper and was tenuously supported by the gold boxes and wrapped straps. Old, time-weakened straps even now stretching and tearing. He heard Niall yell something, felt everything inch upwards.

"Every fucking time," he swore under his breath. "Every god damn fucking time."

Niall's light blinded him again. "What was that?"

The cable jerked and one of the straps parted with a sigh. Two of the boxes plummeted into the abyss. "Lamenting your share, twenty percent doesn't go as far as it used to. Unless you can spend it in Hell."

"You bastard," scowled the Tinker. "That better be a jest."

"Ha, hardly. Don't see you taking any chances. Toss me that netting. And tell Trace to bloody slow down, all this jerking around is a killer." Sol twisted a hand through another loop, swearing when the treasure trove lurched up another foot and almost dislodged him.

The light disappeared and a moment later the netting dropped over him. Sol draped it around and under the pallet the best he could and tied the corners to the winch cable. Not much of a stopgap, but it just needed to hold for a couple more minutes. The edge of the shaft was less than six feet away, so he wrapped a shrieking leg round the cable and reached to pull himself up.

"Could use some help here," he snapped at Niall. But instead of a firm grasp, something stabbed through his hand and he slipped back onto the pallet. What the fuck? Another damn boobytrap? Blood gushed from his palm, he looked up in time to see a clawed foot connect with his throat. Reeling, the next kick caught him above the eye, adding a new constellation to the heavens. Sol sagged onto the pallet, gripping the cable. Tried to get his bearings. Something dropped down behind him, causing the pallet to sway wildly.

A blade went into his forearm, between the bones, and he screamed through his bruised throat. He lashed out with an elbow, striking only air.

"Too late, my ugly friend." Niall whispered into his ear. "Yonder shaft drops three hundred feet into a river with no known beginning nor end. A real underworld situation, perfect for you. And don't you worry, I'll take care of Trace, gratis."

The blade twisted, grating against bone. The pallet jerked up another few inches. Trace. He weirdly wasn't worried about that particular threat at this particular moment. The pain brought a clarity of focus. He couldn't see shit in the near dark, blood running down his forehead and into his eyes. But he could feel Niall's hot onion breath against his cheek. Like the enraged wolf he was, Sol whipped his head around, jaws opening wide, to clamp on to the Tinker's ear.

Teeth sawed through waxy cartilage. Blood spurted. Niall roared and let go.

Sol forced himself up with a twist, smashed his elbow into the man's groin and stomach. Niall slumped, teetered, and toppled, howling into the abyss.

Sol slid back to his knees, feebly clinging to the cable. He couldn't see shit. Couldn't breathe. Couldn't think. The pallet jerked again and the boxes beneath his feet shifted as another strap broke, then another, boxes shifting to strain against the camo netting. One thought reached his lizard brain. Sol slid down the blood slicked cable, tried to get his leg, in or through anything as the netting stretched and threatened to tear. If the cable came off everything, maybe, just maybe he could hang onto the loop.

"Sol!" The voice seemed far away. "Grab the rope."

Something rough bounced off his jack hammering head. Musty hemp. He wound the better of his two arms around it, felt it grow tight. No way. Trace wasn't strong enough to pull him up. Two hundred and twenty pounds of dead weight. Mostly dead weight. Yet somehow, silently screaming, he got a grip and helped drag himself up and over the edge.

Water splashed against his face and beautiful eyes filled his vision. Arms wrapped him.

Tangled hair lashed him. Lips smashed his. He wanted to crush her in his arms, kiss her back, but his body merely quivered.

"I'll take that apology now," she whispered, her forehead touching his. "Out with it."

Sol turned to eject the ear clogging his mouth. Coughed. Rasped out a "Gonna open a bar with this gold. Thinking house special is going to be a sour ear cocktail."

"Jesus, Sol."

"When I said you were a monster, I kinda meant that as a colloquialism, not a challenge," said Bart.

"What we've got ear is a failure to communicate." Sol reached a shaky hand over to yank Niall's knife from his arm. "From ear to eternity." Felt Trace stop him. One pun to many?

"Idiot. Leave it in until I can fix you up. Which is after we get this gold out. Just a few more feet." She kissed him again, nowhere near his frothy lips, and walked to the Chief. Flipped on the winch. It ratcheted a couple more feet of cable and stopped, motor whining.

"Probably caught on the edge," Sol wheezed and levered himself into a sitting position. "I'll get it."

"On your back Solomon Black. And don't make me tell you a second time." She jogged to the cave mouth, got her hands on the cable. Heaved.

The winch motor squealed, smoke pouring out. Metal shrieked. Tore.

"Merciful shit," howled Bart. "Duck and cover, kids!"

The back of the Chief shuddered and burst, fiberglass and rust eaten steel erupting like a junkyard volcano.

Sol flopped back to the ground and Trace flung herself out into the tailing piles as the entire back end of the Chief flew into the tunnel to follow the gold down the shaft.

Trace knocked a knuckle against the hastily spraypainted plywood serving as the new and not so improved rear of the Chief. "See, you can barely tell the difference."

"I…" Sol took a deep breath, let it out slowly. His soul screamed not to die on this hill, but boy his mind sure wanted to. On the bright, side he'd scored new body panels and a tune up. And rid himself of yet another unpleasant fragment of Trace's past. Too bad about the gold though. So much for Dawson City and sour toe cocktails. Had to be a curse. He shrugged, an action that hurt in more ways than one.

"You know what we need?" asked Trace, sliding over and pulling his head down to kiss him.

"Vegreville," he mumbled, peeling his mouth off hers. "Best RV wreckers I know of. That you haven't murdered. Yet."

"We need a goddamn vacation. Bars. Hotels. Exotic food. Exotic pleasures. Haunted bookstores. I know just the place."

"And how, little fancy ass, are we going to accomplish that? We're skint and Niall apparently didn't have an accessible red cent to his name."

Trace purred like a hot kitty and went to where Bart was perched on Niall's rocking chair, holding her hand under his mouth. "Spit it out, trout."

The fish retched twice, disgorging a large nugget Sol recognized as the one he'd snagged on his reconnaissance mission. No wonder the ugly angler had been blissfully silent.

"So," Bart said, no longer ball-gagged with a chunk of gold. "When do we leave?"

POETRY SLAM RESULTS

TENANT ASSOCIATION

Arya Hermione Everdeen: Terrace V intern and Emcee

Thank you for remaining (mostly) seated as you enjoyed/endured the last seven hours. Now for the moment you've been waiting for. After careful deliberation, several recounts, and a lengthy conference between myself and Jan (ultraviolent river otter, lauded poet, judge, sponsor, contestant, executive director, Terrace V rep, my boss) we have a winner! And more importantly, several losers.

Since you've suffered enough, I'll keep this brief and limited to the highlights.

In seventh place, our number one loser is (sorry Terry)...

Terry the Fat Shark: Terrace VI

In a highly unorthodox judgment, our first runner up is...

Percy Bysshe Shelley: Non-contestant

Honourable Mention goes to...

Edward Gorey: Assistant Drive-Thru Manager at Nihilist Arby's

And in first place...

Gary?

Um, yes gentlecritters, it seems we have a ringer—and to be clear, I had nothing to do with this—our Poetry Slam Winner is Gary the Lusty Penguin: Terrace VII.

Wow, okay. Uh, please, let's give a hand to all contestants and—Jan, wait! This wasn't my fault—well, yeah it was rigged because you rigged it—calm down a second, you can't just shoot the...

Gary: Terrace VII rep, Tenants' Association President, and Slam Champion

That's a wrap, folks! Thank you for this ultimately meaningless honour. Afterparty will be held at the Earthly Paradise rooftop pool.

Jan, when you're quite finished here, please have Terry washed and brought to my private chambers.

PURGATORIO TOWERS GAZETTE

TENANT ASSOCIATION

Social Committee

As the Solstice approaches there are several volunteer positions to be filled.

- Feeding of the Night Blooming Tulip (kindly put your affairs in order prior to signing up for this position)
- Yule Log smuggling
- Yule Lad Erotic Revue
- Dinner with Ded Moroz
- Mari Lwyd march for diabetes
- The Mummers: Coercion vs. Consent, a free educational webinar

Special Announcements

Local Beaver goes Mercenary! Scout-Fig Fennel has temporarily stepped down as acting Terrace IV floor rep to explore freelance opportunities. They haven't gotten out of bed in three days but is looking for intriguing characters to interview for their upcoming podcast.

Restrictions Lifted! With the Great Malignancy passing into the Great Apathy, the screaming from beneath the concrete floor of the Basement Commons—which continued at length until mysteriously ceasing and in fact was found never to have been heard at all—has been replaced by a text to speech reading of a LinkdIn article by Factory CEO, [Name Redacted], extolling the virtues of back to office. Extroverts and middle management are asked to amplify this message by honking the words "CULTURE" and "COLLABORATION" at anyone within harassing distance.

Hexavalent vaccinations now available to all residents at any Office Depot throughout the Office Depot District as well as Nihilist Arby's (curly fries sold separately).

Factory Overstock Sale!

Affiliate outlet Jolly Rogers' Fish Emporium is clearing out several tanks of beautiful Tetras. Extra buoyant. All sales final.

Antique doors. Add some rustic charm to your reno with beautiful, reclaimed wood. [Warning: opening door may lead to moderate flaying, billionairage, and intimate discord]

Poets–miserable, pitiable, collectable–and while we can agree that decorating torture chambers with poets does enliven a dungeon or lair, caring for the tormented creatures can be somewhat of a chore: snapping fingers, wine spills, and endless self-promotion foul the spaces where poets can be stashed, depleting any room of oxygen and delivering grief, and not the good kind that everyone loves. But rejoice, friends! Responding to this very need, the Factory has designed the Versifier Omega™, creating a means for the enlightened to display a favorite haranguer without the upkeep of free-range poets and the horrors of free-verse poetry.

Simply put, Versifier Omega is a geometric diorama that entombs biologically inactive poets inside military-grade Lucite blocks. Poets are abducted from the Factory's infamous open-mic affectionately known as the "Tennyson," and as they reach peak fear, their wild articulations are captured using advanced preservation technology. Each poet is mummified in the Factory's private pyramid and pumped with overpriced coffee, break line fluid, and industrial grade cosmetics to make them look successful, well loved, and life-like.

This month's special, a four-pack containing the Spoken Word Artist, Monkey Poet, Pastoralist, and the rare, and always in demand, Gentleman Poet-Musician is currently available for the low price of $99 including shipping.

The Small Print: The Factory advises against storing a Versifier in direct sunlight and warns purchasers to not pour wine, especially Rosé, over their Versifiers as this could lead to condensation, fungal infestation, and existential angst leakage. Not returnable. No refunds.

In Memoriam

Arya Hermione Everdeen. 2001-2022 expired suddenly, and violently, of what the necropsy determined to be extra-unnatural causes. A soul known for her sainted patience and work ethic, she was taken too soon and yet, according to her, not soon enough. A moment of silence will be held at the East Wailing Shrine at 7 a.m. on Friday morning. Regularly scheduled garbage collection will not be affected. Resurrection TBD.

Personals

Hiring: Intern for Terrace V. The successful applicant will have thinly veiled ambition to supplant the existing floor rep, a glancing tolerance for poetry, be available twenty-nine hours per day, and have experience working in fast paced environments, scheduling large teams, and communicating across five to seven disparate instant messaging platforms. This position is unpaid, likely temporary, and duties are subject to change/termination based on the needs of the organization. Reply to:
jan.TerraceV @ PurgatorioTowers.purgatory.

The Librarian is accepting donations of new and gently used memories.

Hound seeks Hare, DM for details. Totally not for murder.

Summer Sisters Pool Maintenance. Service with a big toothy smile and an itsy-bitsy bikini. Book your spring cleaning today!

Buy/Sell/Swap

For Sale: Rolex, Tiffany cufflinks, and one gold molar for sale. Don't ask, won't tell. No reasonable offers refused.

Wanted: Rear assembly for a 76′ D-23 Chieftain. Can pay in gold.

For Sale: 1991 vintage Gibson Explorer. Slightly singed.

Lost and Found

Missing: One larval scarabaeiform identifiable by dull white, black flecked skin and thoroughly unpleasant disposition. May be writhing. When located please keep away from accessible orifices and immediately secure with eldritch bonds and return to Howard Sutter at the Sutter's Rest in Port Urabus. Substantial reward provided.

Funnies

MONEY CAN'T BUY HAPPINESS
GOLD
I FEEL HAPPIER ALREADY!
COPYRIGHT © 2022 ONE-HANDED NIHILISM

PENITENTS

Taija Morgan ("Gold Digger") is a professional fiction editor with short stories and non-fiction articles published in various anthologies and magazines, such as *Opal Writers' Magazine*, the Aurora-nominated *Prairie Gothic* anthology (2020) and *Prairie Witch* anthology (2022) from Prairie Soul Press, Tales to Terrify's horror podcast, and When Words Collide's *In Places Between* anthology (2019). She has bachelor's degrees in psychology and sociology that contribute realism and insight to her dark, twisted fiction.

Chris Marrs ("Pieces of Prue") lives in Calgary, Alberta where it's a lot drier and colder than the West Coast she's used to. She's had short stories published in various anthologies, most notably the Bram Stoker award winning *The Library of the Dead* (edited by

Michael Bailey 2015) and the Bram Stoker award nominated *A Darke Fantastique* (Edited by Jason Brock 2014). She's an active member of the Horror Writers Association. You can find her lurking on Facebook at www.facebook.com/chris.marrs.14, on Twitter as @Chris_Marrs, or Instagram as hauntedmarrs.

Chris Patrick Carolan ("The Envoy's Blessing") is an author, editor, and hovercraft enthusiast, originally from Glasgow but currently based in Calgary, Alberta. He writes science fiction, fantasy, horror, and steampunk, though he has also been known to turn to crime to make ends meet. Crime fiction, that is. *The Nightshade Cabal* was published by Parliament House Press in 2020 and was a finalist for the Crime Writers of Canada Awards of Excellence 'Best First Novel' award. He can be found on Twitter as @cpcwrites but consider this fair warning… it's mostly just wisecracks about McNuggets.

Lindsay Thomas ("Hares and Hounds"). Hailing from the deepest bowels of Alberta, Lindsay traversed the craggy depths of Europe and Asia before bumbling her way into Calgary after The Great Personal Upheaval of 2007. In 2022 she bumbled her way back out again with an unexpected relocation to Bragg Creek, where she resides with her spouse and many canine companions. A perpetual student, Lindsay has degrees in theatre and psychology, and is currently studying the terrestrial art of horticulture. She is a tender of gardens and composer of nonsense who spends her time finding more questions than answers.

Shane Kroetsch ("Attachment") writes stories to explore the inherent darkness that makes us human and the monsters that haunt our dreams. In his spare time, he builds projects out of old junk, paints watercolour blanket ghosts, and shakes his butt while vinyl spins. In addition to publishing a collection of short fiction and a zombie outbreak trilogy, Shane's work is featured in Lampblack Books' *The Planchette Volume One: Genesis* and the Alexandra Writers' Center Society's 40th Anniversary Anthology *WonderShift*. You can read more of his writing and keep up to date with his creative shenanigans at ShaneKroetsch.com and @shanekroetsch.

Sarah L. Pratt (curator) is a curly hair gladiator, ultramarathoner, literary events wrangler, and misfit fictioneer. Her stories have appeared in *Vastarien, NoSleep, Thirteen, On Spec, Shock Totem, Crossed Genres, Year's Best Hardcore Horror Vol. 2* (Red Room Press), and the Bram Stoker Award nominated *Dark Visions 1* (Grey Matter Press) and *Twisted Book of Shadows* (Haverhill Press). She's the author of *Suicide Stitch: Eleven Tales* (EMP Publishing), and co-author of *Terrace VII: Wall of Fire* and *Terrace VI: Forbidden Fruit* (The Seventh Terrace).

Find Sarah on Twitter @The7thTerace or at www.the-seventh-terrace.com

Robert Bose (curator) has a fondness for cosmic horror, sword and sorcery, pulp adventure, and expensive Bourbon, not necessarily in that order. He's the editor and co-publisher of various crime, pulp, and horror books and anthologies—formerly for Coffin Hop Press and currently for The Seventh Terrace. He's also the author of various stories and books including the collections, *Fishing with the Devil, Terrace VII: Wall of Fire* and *Terrace VI: Forbidden Fruit* (the latter two with Sarah L. Pratt). When not writing, editing, publishing, reading, and running ultramarathons, he spends his time pestering his troublesome children, and working as a Chief Architect for an economic forecasting software company.

Find Robert on Twitter @RobBose, on FB at www.facebook.com/robertbose, or at his website at www.robertbose.com.

The Seventh Terrace

Visit us online at
www.the-seventh-terrace.com

ALSO AVAILABLE FROM THE SEVENTH TERRACE

Hell Hath No Sorrow like a Woman Haunted

Unfortunate Elements of My Anatomy

The Walking Son

Starseed

End of the Loop

Trace & Solomon: Torrington

Terrace VI: Forbidden Fruit

Terrace VII: Wall of Fire

The Black City Beneath

Infractus

Suicide Stitch

Fishing with the Devil

Futility: Orange Planet Horror

Terrace VII: Wall of Fire
By Sarah L. Pratt and Robert Bose

Welcome to the Seventh Terrace of Dante's tower of Purgatory. Here, in darkness lit by a wall of flame, you will find souls enslaved by lust. Desire, curdled with madness and desperation. Lust is a chameleon. Enough like love to be deadly. Enough like death to be beautiful. A lonely hunger, eternally

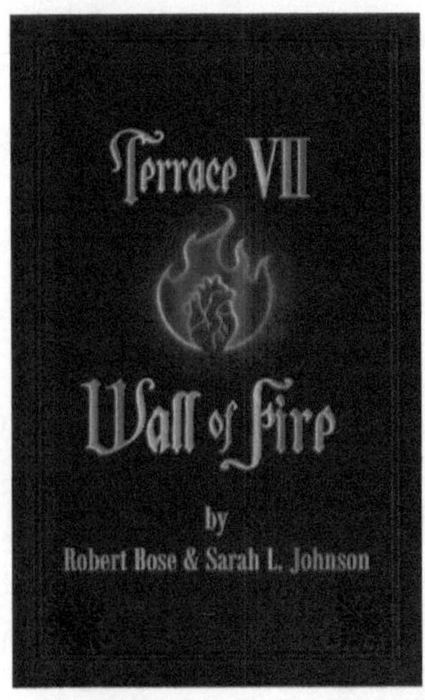

burning in the shadow of what you want, but cannot quite have. From a pair of crazy-in-love criminals on a scavenger hunt at the outskirts of Hell, to a custodian working in a love doll brothel, to a sinister lingerie boutique behind a red door. This collection of dark tales will tempt you down a mere handful of the many paths leading to the wall of fire.

Terrace VI: Forbidden Fruit
Curated by Sarah L. Pratt and Robert Bose

Welcome to the Sixth Terrace of Dante's tower of Purgatory, serving up sins of gluttony in an eternal banquet. On this carefully curated menu you'll find children stuffing themselves to death, wealthy socialites revel in an orgiastic alien feast, and the end of days as seen through an apocalyptic carnival of

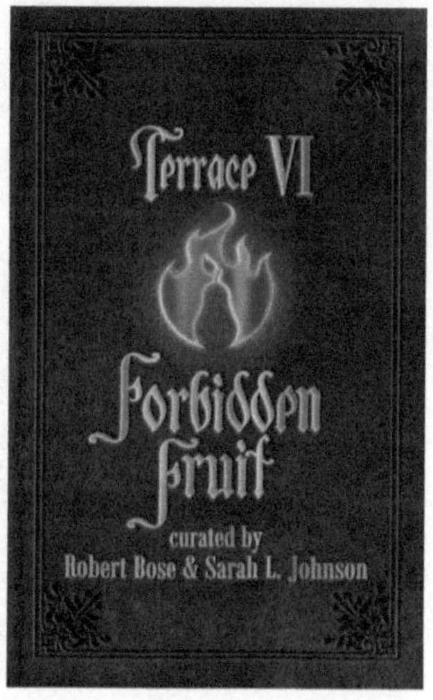

indulgence. Excessive consumption also manifests in darker hungers, for cruelty, for distraction, or possession. A pair of grifters bent on having it all chase a Scottish leprechaun across the English countryside, a newly deceased addict vies for the attention of Heavenly Higher Ups, and degenerate poker players gamble with unforeseen currency it's just the beginning.

Featuring stories and art by Mike Thorn, Robin van Eck, Eddie Generous, Cam Hayden, Julie Hiner, Konn Lavery, Sarah L. Pratt (Johnson) and Robert Bose.

Unfortunate Elements of My Anatomy
By Hailey Piper

Love twisted into horrific shapes, nightmares driven by cruel music, and a world where what little light remains fractures the sky into midnight rainbows in eighteen stories tracing the dark veins of queer horror, isolation, and the monstrous feminine. The universe unwinds to the tune of a malicious ice cream truck

jingle in "We All Scream". "The Law of Conservation of Death" dictates that a ghost pursue his prey across her every reincarnation. Superstitions thrive even in the distant future and across the stars when a colony shuttle mounts a witch trial in "Hairy Jack". And try to "Forgive the Adoring Beast" as it scavenges a world of dead gods for tokens of bloody affection. Including two new short stories and a never-before-published novelette, *Unfortunate Elements of My Anatomy* digs deep inside and clings to the beating nightmare heart you always knew was there.

Hell Hath No Sorrow like a Woman Haunted
By RJ Joseph

The Black women in these tales are women we all know. The mothers, wives, business owners, creatives, and more, that we see in everyday life. They perform the impossible and hold all ends together.

Sometimes, they're an open book, their stories written in the

beloved lines of their faces and the varied bodies they wear with pride or weariness.

Other times, their secrets squirm beneath the surface, aching for release and discovery while beckoning others to lean in. They whisper the horror of their predicaments, closer to home than you realize.

These Black women are more than we know. They're also victims, monsters…and often, a little of both.

Starseed
By Stephen Guy

In a world illuminated by gaslight, a wealthy, debauched dandy's mentor tests the limits of conscience with a series of human-alien hybridization experiments, facilitated by the decryption of a forbidden text now known as the Voynich Manuscript.

Not knowing what it is they've unleashed, mayhem ensues, with hired killers, Brazilian Wandering Spiders, and shady professionals willing to undertake the performance of any act that one should be ashamed to ask for. There is flesh, and the power that holds. Juices run, blood flows, and ichor oozes. The dandy soon comes to learn that wealth cannot buy love, the past exists for nothing so much as to haunt the present, and as long as there is desire, the Star Flower will procure what it needs to bloom and spread its seed through the cosmos.